SKOTOS – The End of Darkness

BROOKS

Copyright© 2022

by

Dr. Steven Brooks

Published by Professional Employee Training Services LLC
Weslaco, Texas.

All Rights Reserved.

This book is a work of fiction and includes references to historical events for chronological reference and additional information for dramatic purposes. Names, characters, businesses, organizations, places, events, and incidents are the product of the author's imagination and are fictitious. Any resemblance to actual persons, living or dead, events, or locations is entirely coincidental. If the depiction of certain events has resulted in similarities with history, these similarities are neither intended nor coincidental but inevitable. All characters and events in this book, even those based on actual people, are entirely for entertainment and purely fictional.

No portion of this book may be reproduced, stored in a retrieval system, or transmitted in any form or by any means—electronic, mechanical, photocopy, recording, scanning, or other—except for brief quotations in critical reviews or articles, without prior written permission from the author.

ISBN: 9798391706748

DEDICATION

To Everyone Who Encouraged and Believed in Me…Thank You!

To Everyone Who Purchased the First and Second Books…Thank You!

SPECIAL THANKS

To Angela Mendoza, my wonderful set of second eyes, for taking the time to review the content.

VETERAN-OWNED and VETERAN SUPPORTERS

As a veteran, I have teamed up with the *Wounded Warrior Project,* and a portion of my book sales are donated. Join me in supporting America's brave men and women!
https://support.woundedwarriorproject.org

PROUD SUPPORTER
WOUNDED WARRIOR PROJECT

Join me in supporting our youngest members who fight individual battles. https://www.stjude.org

St. Jude Children's Research Hospital

FROM THE AUTHOR

"Not everything is as it seems because perspectives change everything, and everything is interpreted by perspectives." - Dr. Steven Brooks

"Time is endless until you end." - Dr. Steven Brooks

"Light will always penetrate the darkness." – JC

"The breadth, depth, and scope of reality are based upon the human experience... Κατανοώντας τη ζωή" - Dr. Steven Brooks

"Three may keep a secret, if two of them are dead." - Ben Franklin

"Darkness cannot drive out darkness; only light can do that." - Martin Luther King, Jr.

TABLE OF CONTENTS

FLASHBACK - Prologue 6
THE VAULT - Chapter 1 9
THE OFFICE - Chapter 2 12
ANXIETY - Chapter 3 15
WELCOME HOME - Chapter 4 19
UNFAMILIAR TERRITORY - Chapter 5 24
HUDDLE - Chapter 6 31
ARISTOCRACY OR ANARCHY? - Chapter 7 38
PERKS AND QUIRKS - Chapter 8 43
UNEXPECTED HISTORY - Chapter 9 49
DID HE NOTICE? - Chapter 10 53
BREAKFAST - Chapter 11 57
RENEWED FOCUS - Chapter 12 66
INNOCENCE LOST - Chapter 13 74
BREAKFAST – Chapter 14 83
CLEAN UP - Chapter 15 87
CONNECTIONS - Chapter 16 92
HIDDEN TREASURES - Chapter 17 96
SURPRISE - Chapter 18 109
NEXT - Chapter 19 119
NICE TO MEET YOU - Chapter 20 124
SUPRISE - Chapter 21 131
PLANS - Chapter 22 145
MISSING - Chapter 23 148
AWAKENING – Chapter 24 155

TAKEN - Chapter 25 165
AWAKENING - Chapter 26 168
QUESTIONS - Chapter 27 177
REVELATION - Chapter 28 180
GONE - Chapter 29 192
THE HUNT BEGINS - Chapter 30 198
TOOLS OF THE TRADE - Chapter 31 202
NEW RULES - Chapter 32 210
CONTACT - Chapter 33 213
ONE CHANCE - Chapter 34 217
Epilogue 232

FLASHBACK - Prologue

Bobby sat in the back seat, looking over his shoulder. He hadn't experienced a surge of adrenaline of that magnitude since combat. The driver spoke. "Are you ok, Colonel Arrollos?"

Even amid the chaos, Bobby recognized his new identity, which could only mean one thing. Albright contacted the extraction team and began the transition process for him to resume his prior duties on the 12th floor under the title of his new identity. He was prepared to update the team on the mission, his name change, and his assignment as a Spanish officer engaged in counterespionage. Outside of these issues, everything would resume as normal.

The passenger looked over his shoulder. "Sir, we have you. I will guarantee that nothing will happen to you. This vehicle is fully armored to withstand all small and medium-caliber weapons." Bobby smiled, knowing the escorts did not know his abilities and experiences. "Thank you. I appreciate your confidence and skills. By the way, I see from your choice of weapon, the suppressed HK 91, which you are carrying, you prefer it over the suppressed M4! I like the 7.62 over the 5.56 myself." The extraction team exchanged glances as they realized their passenger was not a typical soft target.

After twenty minutes of driving using a series of zigzags with stop-and-go actions, they arrived at the Smithsonian. Before departing, the three men scanned the area for questionable people or threats. Everything was clear. Bobby was excited and thanked them for keeping him safe. Soon afterward, he was standing in the doorway of Albright's office. Albright was expecting him. "Welcome home. How was your day?"

Bobby grinned. "Outside of watching someone kill themselves and a three-member team of blood-thirsty crazies trying to kill me, it was the same as always...boring!" They laughed together. Bobby sat and sighed. "Thanks for sending the pickup team. What a day! I never expected this. What's your feedback?"

Albright nodded. "No problem. Your words are an understatement of what you experienced. I'll bet you haven't had that much excitement since Afghanistan. I'm glad you are here. Now that you are safe, our next step is to get you back in the saddle on the 12th floor. Your first mission is to get everyone on board and up to speed."

Bobby smiled. "Isn't that the truth? So, where and when do I start? Who should I contact?"

"I'll take care of the preliminaries. You will report tomorrow and resume your duties just as you had before the incident. Except you will be in Spanish military casual."

"Incident? Is that what you call it?"

Albright nodded. "Until further notice, it was an incident. I will send you a secure e-mail that you will review and share with the team tomorrow afternoon. I don't want to keep them in suspense for too long. That's how rumors start."

"I understand. The more the teams know, the better. I agree. I will do as you order. By the way, I don't have any Spanish military casual clothing."

"Yes, you do. There is a box on the floor next to your desk with five complete sets of casual attire."

"I should have known. You are always one step ahead. Thank you. Anything else?"

Albright nodded his head. "Keep me posted."

"I'll head over to the vault and join Marty. By the way, how is Dr. Martinez doing?"

"She is doing better. Thanks for asking. I'm sure Marty is looking forward to your company. She enjoys working with you, but I'm sure she isn't going to be happy working without you." Bobby grimaced and left the office.

Albright picked up his cell phone and dialed. The voice acknowledged the connection. "Dr. Albright, to what do I owe the privilege?"

"We need to start *Operation Broken Vessel*."

For a minute, there was silence. "Ok. I will notify the team of your request. Are you authorizing me to proceed?"

"Yes. Thank you. I will update you in a few days. Goodbye." Albright hung up and sat with his fingers interlocked before him. He was pensive.

PART ONE

OPERATION BROKEN VESSEL

THE VAULT - Chapter 1

Marty was reviewing the documents and writing an outline of the information when Bobby walked in. She looked up and a smile immediately filled her face. "Hey, stranger. How are you doing?"

"I was only gone for one day!"

Marty sat. "Yes, one day, which almost resulted in your last day. Albright filled me in. You are one lucky man."

"Blessed! I am blessed. Yes, I haven't experienced that much juice in my bloodstream since the day I was hit."

"Juice?"

Bobby smiled. "Adrenaline. It was an incredible flashback combined with real-time insanity."

"I cannot imagine anything of that magnitude. Life and death stand before you and one will step forward to embrace you."

Bobby was expressionless. "That was incredible. I've never thought of it from that perspective. What an insightful metaphor. I will share that with my counselor when we meet again."

"Your counselor?"

Bobby nodded. "Yes, my post-combat counselor. Sometimes, I experience post-traumatic episodes when I'm sleeping or whenever something triggers a flashback. I've been doing much better."

"I'm so glad to hear that. I did not know."

Bobby nodded. "Most people don't know, but active-duty soldiers and veterans keep things deep-sixed in fear of being seen as weak. This is especially true of the Spec-Ops warriors."

"When did you realize you needed someone to talk to somebody?"

"When I returned to Bragg, I was recovering in the hospital and one night I awoke in a cold sweat reliving a down range moment. I told my doctor, and she recommended I visit the *Embedded Behavioral Health* (EBH) Center."

"Did it help?"

Bobby smiled. "More than I could have imagined. I never realized there were several of these care centers at Bragg and most military bases. They are near the units and have an open-door policy. Anyone can tell their supervisor and walk in the front door without questions. The accessibility removes the stigma associated with feeling like a failure or weak."

"That's incredible. I'm so glad it helped you and is available to other members of the military."

> *"It seems somebody at the Army Medical College finally did something right!"*

Marty rolled her eyes. "Is that sarcasm?

Bobby looked down and up. "Yes. For years, veterans have felt they didn't matter after walking out of the uniform or off the battlefield. This is a welcome treatment for us. I guess I shouldn't be negative. Unfortunately, it makes me mad that so many have taken their lives because of that mindset. I've lost a couple of battle buddies to suicide, and it hurts deeply. It's another wound to the ones they leave behind because we feel we failed them. Didn't do enough. Survivor's guilt sucks!"

Marty saw the tears form in Bobby's eyes. "I'm sorry. I try to understand, but I cannot fathom what our warriors feel."

"Thank you. I'll be ok. My goals in life are to successfully complete every mission regardless of where it is and help others."

"Wonderful! How about we switch gears? What is next on your agenda?"

Bobby sighed. "I will return to the 12th floor, and you will continue to review the documents and record anything you feel needs to be shared with me. I am your other set of eyes and ears. We are still battle buddies."

Marty smiled, knowing the gravity of Bobby's words. He would say nothing of that magnitude unless she earned it. "I am humbled. Thank you. I'll miss you and your smell."

Bobby was surprised. "Me and my smell? What's that all about?"

Marty looked serious. "Your smell. Nobody ever told you about your smell?"

"No. Are you saying I stink?"

"Yes!"

"What the heck?"

"You also skink at recognizing when I poke fun at you!" Marty burst into laughter. After a second, her words registered, and Bobby laughed. "You stink as a friend to even mess with my self-consciousness like that."

"You will recover."

"Maybe I won't miss you as much as I thought. Should I recant my earlier words?"

"No! I earned them! Anyway, we will review the documents every day."

Bobby smiled. "Yep! We will. Let me take off and get into the 12th-floor storm and quell the waves."

"Have a great day. I'll see you later tonight. Tada!"

"Tada to you too!" Bobby exited the vault and Marty resumed her investigation and interrogation of the documents.

THE OFFICE - Chapter 2

He sat with his back to the door, looking out the window. This was his daily routine when stress overwhelmed him. He became one with nature. He did this every day. This was his break time to step away from the hustle and bustle of everything. He sat in the serenity of quietness, taking in the respite when he was interrupted by a knock on the door. The door slowly opened as a man spoke. "Sir. I have an important message and please allow me to apologize for the interruption, but it's from the Chinese ambassador."

Without turning his head, he called out. "Come in. Let's get this addressed so I can resume my mental playtime. What's up?"

"I don't know if you are aware, but yesterday, two Chinese nationals were being monitored by our FBI agents for espionage, and the situation escalated."

"Escalated? Please define escalated."

"When the FBI agents closed in for the arrest, one of the Chinese nationals took a pistol from an FBI agent and killed himself. The other man took off running and was taken into custody and arrested. Now, the Chinese are demanding the deceased man's body be released to the embassy. Unfortunately, we have a situation with that."

"Situation? What is the issue?"

"The dead man is an active member of our military and a naturalized citizen."

"Do we have to release his body to the Chinese?"

"Only if his wife or parents request it."

"Is he married?"

"No, sir."

"Are his parents requesting his remains?"

"His parents are both deceased."

He spun around in his chair. "Then we keep the body. Understood?"

"Yes, sir. We also need to address the other situation regarding the other man who we incarcerated. The

Ambassador is demanding his immediate release. They are accusing us of arresting a Chinese nationalist without having evidence or due process. They are requesting a *Writ of Habeas Corpus*."

"How would they know there's no evidence?"

"Sir, it's obvious they know what these two men were doing, and the first thing any nation does is deny culpability, especially with espionage."

"Exactly! And the second thing done is we refuse to show them the body until our investigation is complete. Let's hold the guy for a week and if nothing comes up, we release him. If we discover something, we will be glad we kept him in custody. If not, he would be in China free from prosecution. Has any of this made the news?"

"No. We have kept a lid on it until you were notified. What is the next step regarding the press release?"

"Let's keep it out of the spotlight for now. The Chinese will not involve the media because they will be scrutinized harshly and suspected of espionage. Let's regroup in 48 hours. Thank you for keeping me informed."

"Yes, sir. There is another issue I just received to share with you. It's from the DoD."

"What does the *Department of Defense* want now?"

"Sir, they don't want anything. They are informing us of a joint venture with Spain. Since the fiasco at the safe building's 12th-floor with the comatose patients and now the Chinese espionage issue, they requested assistance from Spain."

"Why Spain?"

"Spain has a top-notch computer guru who has the experience that aligns with the vacancy created by the breach and unexpected vacancy. This is a Top-Secret Umbra slot and selection which is an under-the-radar agreement that will strengthen our military relationship with Spain."

"Is the Spaniard cleared to work with us?"

"Yes! He is scheduled to report tomorrow. Do you have any objections or concerns?"

"No. Keep me posted on any issues that arise in the future. We cannot afford to have another issue with that branch, especially now, because it has gone international."

"Yes, sir. I will now excuse myself." He nodded and turned his chair to the window, then resumed his respite of relaxation, staring at the sky. After the interruption, he regained his attention on a bird as it gracefully soared invisibly suspended beneath the cloudless blue sky high above the trees. This distracted his attention, and the strained concentration waned from his face while watching the bird's outstretched wings lift it high above the ocean of humanity teeming with problems, causing him to envy the bird's worry-free existence. As always, he was jealous of the bird; these thoughts were an everyday occurrence.

ANXIETY - Chapter 3

His breathing was heavy as he completed the stress test. The 60-year-old was in excellent condition as he wiped the sweat from his face with a hand towel. "What's the status of the search? What have you heard from the Black Widow?"

"Sir, she contacted me yesterday and seems to have arrived at an impasse."

"We are not paying her for an impasse. I want results. What is her plan to get around the roadblock?"

"She said her resources have dried up. She understands the importance of finding Albright and his documents. She is continuing her efforts."

He frowned. "Efforts? Whatever! I need answers and a shower. Meet me in my office in one hour."

"Yes, sir. See you there."

Kuka was talking to DeLorean on the cell phone. She was concerned she would fail this mission. If so, it would be her first. She was world-renowned as one of the best operators in the covert operations business. DeLorean assured her she would be fine. Her assets were dedicated and did whatever it took to succeed. There was too much money riding on this mission. Someone was determined to find the documents. Deep pockets told her this was a high-profile organization that wanted to reveal what Albright had recorded. Whatever the documents would reveal, it must be earth-shattering.

Albright's connections assured Bobby's position as Chang's replacement was uneventful. The orders were entered into the DoD system, even though the approving signatures were perfect digital reproductions that passed security. It didn't matter because it was presented to and approved by the Commander-in-Chief, the President; and nobody would dare question it after Executive approval. The mission was to ostensibly use a Spanish Military Commander to help secure network security internationally, but the truth was to find the person or persons trying to locate Albright, and his documents.

Dr. Martinez completed the pamphlets for the Caiaphas event. She loved her responsibility as curator to make history engaging and the event successful. She was relaxing in her office now that everything was complete. When she heard a knock on the door, she took a deep breath and exhaled. She opened her eyes and was greeted by Marty with her million-dollar smile. "It's nice to see you, Marty. To what do I owe your visit?"

"I don't know whom to talk to about a question I have regarding the research of Dr. Albright's documents, but I know you are well-versed in historical events."

Dr. Martinez smiled. "I can't say I have the answer to your question, but share it with me and let's see what we discover."

Marty smiled. "During a conversation with Dr. Albright, he mentioned a hidden message was discovered in the *Dead Sea Scrolls*, which prompted Bobby and me to ask what the message was. I'll never forget how I felt when told it was an end times message. I mean, I've heard the stories and seen the movies, but this hit me hard. I wasn't reading an action book or watching a suspenseful movie. I was sitting in front of a man who had more intelligence and knowledge than I would gain in ten lifetimes. I was stunned."

Dr. Martinez nodded. "Dr. Albright is a wealth of information. I'm curious. What prompted him to tell you this? He is usually reserved and doesn't say anything."

"Bobby noticed my curiosity about the *Rosetta Stone* and the *Dead Sea Scrolls*. He later shared his observations with Albright."

"Yes. It is a secret. However, we are not completely convinced that it contains the end-of-times message, but there seems to be a message of grave concern. I couldn't resist the pun. How about this? I'll keep you posted should we discover more details about it."

"Thank you. I appreciate your time and explanation. I feel relieved."

"There's no reason to be anxious. It won't give you another second of life. Live each day as though it will be your last, because one day will be the last."

> *"I get scared when I think about the apocalypse. I'm not ready to die."*

"Few of us are. Just relax. We will talk later. Have a wonderful day."

"Thank you, Dr. Martinez. I appreciate your kindness." Marty returned to the vault and resumed her review of Albright's documents.

Bobby returned to his office and opened the box. The Spanish casual attire was better than he expected. In fact, he was impressed. Today was unknown, with the possibility of confusion, enlightenment, and epiphanies. As an officer, Bobby's primary duties were to ensure the safety of his personnel, and the mission was never compromised; however, this venture was taking them into dangerous territory. Nothing could be taken for granted.

The hour passed quickly, and they met in the office. The 60-year-old began the conversation. "I have been advised that our team failed to terminate the target. How is it possible that three experts with weapons could not take out one unarmed man?"

"Sir, with all due respect, the situation was compromised because of the environment. We were in an open location teeming with tourists taking photos and videos. When the target evaded our aggression and crashed, all the cameras were trained on him and us. We took the proper evasive actions to avoid detection and identification. We had been compromised and immediately left the area."

"Were you able to determine the status of the target?"

"At that moment, he was still alive. As we drove away, I saw him exit the vehicle while police and bystanders immediately assisted him. I don't know if he was wounded or not."

"Unfortunately, I was informed my hired guns, supposedly some of the best in the world, failed to administer one body shot. The impact of the airbag did more damage."

"I'm sorry. Is there a contingency plan?"

"In my world, there is always a contingency plan! I will meet with you later. Your presence is no longer required. Please leave."

The abruptness wasn't anything new. His attitude was more of a spoiled child instead of a well-known Aristocrat who was one of the richest men in the world. "Of course. Please excuse me." With that, he left the office.

PART TWO

SAME FACE, SAME PLACE

WELCOME HOME - Chapter 4

Bobby walked into the office and was immediately greeted with cheers, pats on the back, and applause. Any reservations he felt the team members may have had were immediately dispelled. After greeting the team, he asked them to meet him in the conference room. A few minutes later, everyone was sitting prepared to hear the details of how their formerly dead commander was resurrected and returned to work as a colonel in the Spanish Military. After Bobby disappeared, everyone shared their perspective of what happened to the Major and why. Now, a few months later, he was sitting with them, totally unexpected and incognito. The overarching question everyone shared was why he disappeared and what brought him back.

Bobby sat in the commander's chair with a big smile on his face. "I am so glad to be back. I know you must have a million questions and I will attempt to answer them today. Which, as you know, means you will be told everything you need to know, and nothing more!" They nodded in agreement.

Martinez shouted. "That's right. Some things never change." They laughed. This was a healing moment for everyone; the air was full of positive energy. The shock of losing a man who was the foundation of their operations and missions took an emotional toll on each, and at this moment, they were experiencing another set of emotions.

"I can't tell you everything, but I will get you up to speed." All eyes were on him. "As you know, I'm not dead. I'm sorry you had to experience the trauma of losing a team member. Believe me, I felt the pain and loss of being stolen from you. As you know, when I was here, our objectives were to protect the complex, the people, and the network. This is still our mission. However, there is a twist to my presence now. I'm sure you all noticed I'm not wearing an American uniform or name tag. This is a Spanish Army casual dress uniform. I am now assigned to Spain as a Commanding Officer, a bird colonel if you can believe that, in charge of network security and covert operations."

Gold raised his hand. "Sir. If I may?" Bobby nodded. "First, congratulations on the promotion from major to Spanish full-bird colonel." The team laughed, knowing their humor would not be taken as sarcasm, but to show solidarity with Bobby.

Bobby laughed. "Yes, that was interesting, but not as interesting as this. I haven't put on my name tag because I wanted to introduce myself. From this moment on, I am now Colonel Roberto Arrollos from the Spanish military assigned to this branch." It was as if everyone were reading a script when they collectively asked, "What?"

"Yes. You are now part of a covert operation with me as the mission specialist. You will address me as Colonel Arrollos to maintain the integrity of our new mission. I'm not demanding this because I am on a power trip. I'm asking because our lives will be in immediate danger if anyone slips up and exposes me. I'm sure you also noticed the change in my hair color and uniform. Your diligence in keeping my new identity secure cannot be stressed enough. Questions?"

Hayes spoke. "Sir, I'm sure I speak on behalf of the team when I promise our dedication to protect you and the integrity of our new mission. I cannot emphasize how elated I am, we are, to have you back. After listening to your words regarding the expectations of this team, I know we are in for one heck of a ride. Glad to have you back."

Bobby nodded in agreement. "Thank you. I know this transition will take some time and until we are completely comfortable with it, we will hold each other accountable. This will help us transition and reprogram who I am, why I am here, and our mission. Now, without further delay, let me get you up to speed. As you remember, our network was being bombarded several times a week by an unknown aggressor. There was speculation this aggressor was receiving some type of assistance in combating our firewall. I was reluctant to consider the perpetrator could have been one of our own. I hand-picked each of you and put my complete trust in everyone. This was my primary aim for each of you. However, there was another mission, *Top-Secret Umbra*, that I was also engaged in. All behind the scenes. It's the reason I disappeared."

Hayes interrupted. "Sir. Isn't *Top-Secret Umbra* used for top-tier secret classifications?"

"Very much so. It's not common knowledge outside of intel services, but it is still the highest order of security. My second operation jeopardized my life and took the life of Nurse Marty Bell from the second floor. I was kidnapped after she was shot." Bobby knew he could not risk exposing Marty, so he stuck to the story she was dead. "That moment was pure insanity and unexpectedly took me away from this team. As you know, the 6th floor is no more. After my disappearance, it was leaked that a drug-induced coma was the tool used to keep patients, former CIA, NSA, and military operatives, imprisoned here without legal due process or notification of kin. This was a nightmare for their families because each disappeared with no trace of what happened to them. There was nothing wrong with any of these people. They were illegally held on the 6th floor until they died."

Gold exclaimed. "Sir, that is unbelievable! Right here under our noses?"

Bobby nodded. "Unfortunately, many things are hidden in plain sight. One of our guests was of the highest order of national security. I cannot say who that person was, but you must trust me. The less you know, the safer you are."

Everyone exchanged glances. Tension filled the air.

"This highest priority person may have been a target, but he disappeared one day without a trace, only to show up a few weeks later for payback. He wanted to make things right for whatever took him out of service. His goal was to find the people who were out to get him and remove them permanently. Since I was unwittingly brought into his situation, I became one of two people who knew of him. I also became part of his master plan to target the domestic enemy and bring them to accountability...if he wanted them to live. Our mission was to find the mole, protect him, protect his documents, and protect our nation. That's all I can tell you. Everything else is beyond your pay grade."

> *This is a need to know when I want you to know the operation.*

"If I don't tell you, don't ask. Is that understood?"
Another collective answer. "Yes, sir."
"Our aim is two-fold. Find whomever Chang was funneling information to and find the domestic enemy. This way, we kill them before they kill us!"
Martinez interrupted. "Kill? What have we gotten ourselves into?"
"Yes, kill. How serious is this? Yesterday, three military-equipped assailants pulled next to me in a black SUV as I was driving and peppered my car with 7.62 armor-piercing rounds. I took evasive measures and crashed into a tree. They took off, and I walked away, but I'm sure they will return. This was not a random attempted carjacking. I don't know why I am their target, but I'm sure we will find out why soon."
Martinez and the others were shocked. "Sir, you said someone is trying to kill you. Do you have any idea if they are after Major Brooks or Colonel Arrollos?"
"That's the million-dollar question. At this point, we cannot assume anything. We must respond as if it is both. Somebody has been given my classified file, and that incriminates the entire system's failure to ensure integrity. This is another stone we must overturn."

Gold. "Have you been assigned a security detail, sir?"

"Yes. The Spanish Ambassador has requested assistance from our military and several federal police agencies."

"Dang it, sir. This is some serious stuff. Is there any danger they may attempt to breach our building?"

"We take no chances! This is more than just a network security mission. Each of you has combat experience and from this day forward, I expect to see you holstering a pistol and strapping a suppressed M4 with no less than ten 30-round magazines. We will meet at the armory immediately after this meeting. Questions? Ok, let's regroup at the armory. Well, done team!"

Martinez looked at Gold. "This is some serious stuff. They may not be aware of our position here, but we will not be surprised. We will take out any trash that comes our way."

Gold. "Cool! Good to know, and good to go!"

Everyone was issued weapons, magazines, and ammunition.

Bobby spoke. "Alright. I will send documents to each of you using the secure email system. These emails are FYEO, for your eyes only, and must never be printed or shared. By the way, I have increased our internal surveillance operations exponentially. Anything you type, email, or save will be critiqued for integrity and mission accountability. Anything that raises a red flag will be immediately addressed. Don't mess up! That's it. Thank you for supporting me and the mission. You are dismissed. Stand by for my email." With that, everyone departed to their offices.

UNFAMILIAR TERRITORY - Chapter 5

DeLorean was not accustomed to his sister being pushed into a corner. In fact, this was a first. Her headstrong determination to succeed at everything propelled her over every obstacle. This situation was unfamiliar territory for both her and him. He was doing everything possible within his branch operations to assist her without raising a red flag. Unfortunately, this venture was not typical in any capacity. This was the highest-profile assignment ever undertaken, and the odds of succeeding seemed to mount against them as each avenue led to a dead end. He was pressuring his team to use every available resource, which included members of the CIA, NSA, MI6, and FBI. Kuka had even reached out to Edward and Julian. The results? Nothing! Even the lead from Kiki regarding the possibility that Marty and Bobby had visited the restaurant went cold. He shared his sister's frustration. He took a brain break, as he called them, to disconnect from the tension, and listened to some instrumental music; he immediately felt the calming effect. Ten minutes of non-job-related activity enveloped in music was his cure-all. He pushed himself away from the desk and stretched his legs as he took a deep breath and slowly exhaled. After a few repetitions, he felt his focus return and grabbed the newspaper, which he purchased earlier when he stopped for coffee. He opened the front page, and the headline caught his eye and attention.

"Assassination Attempt Near Arlington."

What's this all about? He read the details of how a lone driver, the "miracle man," survived an attempt on his life in broad daylight. The photos showed an SUV with a front end looking like Swiss cheese; a visual reminder depicting the gravity of the force used. He knew this was no random case of road rage. No amateur would have a close grouping of rounds directly placed on the engine; the quickest way to disable any vehicle. This was the work of professionals using military-grade weapons. The vehicle was stopped by the barrage of bullets, but why was the target still alive? Was this the correct target? Was the target able to return fire? Were the police in the immediate area? Regardless, this was a planned operation, but not for assassination. He was surprised the assassins had failed to successfully dispose of the soft target. Witnesses said the shooters quickly fled the scene while the man miraculously walked away from the wreckage. No identification of the survivor was given who had been quickly removed from the scene. DeLorean was intrigued that this episode to "rub somebody out" was so close to the middle of commerce. This was very intriguing. Then something caught his eye as he was about to move to the next article. It was one of the witness photos. He meticulously examined each and noticed there was a photo showing the driver, the alleged "miracle man," getting into a black Audi Q7 with men in the front seats. He looked closer. These were escorts, not friends who came to take someone home after an accident because friends in the front passenger seat don't carry a suppressed military-grade weapon. DeLorean was transfixed by the photo. Something else grabbed his attention, but he couldn't place a finger on it. Then he realized the victim had an uncanny resemblance to one deceased Major Robert Brooks, except with a different hair color. Is this an incredible twist of fate? He had to check his emotions and think as a professional. If this was Bobby, why would he be back in DC? Any attempt to hide him in plain sight would go against all Spec-Op protocols. Could this person be a doppelgänger or possibly a decoy? The quality of the photos also raised the question of image integrity, which means the actual photo could be nothing more than a distortion that skewed the image. He needed to get an actual copy of the photograph before doing or thinking anything else. He would contact the news agency. Even though he knew this was against his best interests, he wanted to touch base with Kuka. He took a picture of the photo and sent it with the words, 'Kiki may be right.'

In less than 20 seconds, Kuka called. "Are you serious? Could Bobby be in town…alive? If this is true, then Nurse Bell is probably nearby." Kuka had seen many incidents of plastic surgery and identification changes performed by high-profile targets needing to fly under the radar.

Kuka was back in familiar territory as adrenaline coursed through her body. "Do you have the date and location of the incident?"

DeLorean nodded even though they were on their cell phones. "Yes. Are you going to start contact with your security camera experts in the police department and FBI?"

"You know me, well, brother. I want to see if we can track the vehicle from the incident to their destination. This will provide the opportunity to get a visual of the person and make a positive ID."

DeLorean smiled. "I'll run the tags and see who owns the vehicle. Call me tomorrow afternoon so we can keep each other up to date."

"Sounds like a plan to me. Talk to you tomorrow."

DeLorean heard the change in his sister's voice. Her attitude was positive. Regardless of the outcome, she needed some positive news.

"Kuka."

She paused at the tone of his voice. "Yes."

"Let me remind you, caution you, this is probably a dead end. There are too many open issues regarding the exposure of Major Brooks and the integrity of his operations for this to just fall into our lap. We must be diligent because I know we are not the only people watching and looking for Brooks. This could blow up in our faces, and in my position, I could end up with a court martial and do time at Leavenworth."

Kuka was silent. Her brother's words were like a punch in the gut that immediately took the air out of her. She responded timidly. "I understand. You are watching our best interests. I also know we must investigate this completely to ensure this person is not Brooks."

"I agree. I'll call you later. Let's take small steps so we do not draw any unnecessary attention to our investigation."

They agreed and hung up.

William Martin continued his relentless quest to find additional information regarding Albright and Churchill's undisclosed meeting. The question persisted, "How do I find a connection if I don't know what the connection is?" This consideration was very Socratic, which surprised him with this recollection and the correlation. He laughed, thinking how he never expected to use any philosophical adages learned in college during his tenure as a spy. He regained focus and, for the next two hours, sat at the table in the archive's basement, sifting through page after page for any clues.

Bobby was in the zone. He was searching the computer using Chang's CAC, which provided access to everything Chang did, created, saved, received, sent, and deleted. He had contacted NSA and requested a digital forensic expert to report and perform a binary review of the hard drive to sequentially reconstruct the file allocation table and expose every file Chang touched. As the Spanish attaché for network security, Bobby was provided a new computer system and total network access. His title as a diplomatic and military emissary was the key to getting quick access from the NSA and the use of a forensic expert involved and resources not normally provided for uniformed military members of the U.S. This was the diplomatic golden goose he would milk for everything possible.

A few minutes later, he was interrupted. Martinez knocked on the door frame. "Sir, your guest has arrived." Bobby stood and walked around the desk and met a petite

Air Force sergeant carrying an aluminum case that further emphasized her slight frame. "Thank you for coming. I am Colonel Roberto Arrollos." She extended her hand. "I am sergeant Wanda Striker. Nice to meet you, sir."

Martinez looked over her head at Bobby. "Colonel, isn't that one of the coolest names for a military member involved in counterespionage?"

Bobby nodded in agreement. "It has the ring of 'take no prisoners.' I hope we never offend you, Sergeant Striker."

Wanda laughed. "Not at all! Being my size and having a name that is bigger than life in the military has many advantages and perks. I cannot say how many times someone has mentioned the fortuitous expectation of my name."

Bobby smiled. "On behalf of our agency, thank you for the time and talents you bring to the table. Please don't be offended, but considering the security and intensity of our situation, I must make sure you understand the gravity of your mission and our expectations before you continue."

"I understand. Will you be requiring a signed affidavit from me assuring secrecy?"

"Yes. Will your agency have any issues with that?"

"No, sir. This is a common protocol in the black-ops forensic network security and investigation arena. By the way, after this encounter you can never contact me should any additional issues arise, so make this trip of my services as complete as possible. I'm an asset with strict protocols."

"Outstanding. I understand and appreciate your transparency. Thank you for the details you provided me. We had a former team member, the owner of this computer, meet with one of your NSA members a few weeks ago. We were not briefed on the purpose or subject of their meeting, which is why you are here today. I'm hoping you will discover answers to my questions."

Wanda nodded. "Not a problem, sir. In our business, we don't ask, we don't tell, and we say nothing; yet, after we leave, information magically appears. I guess that's the wonderful treasure provided by Op-Sec gurus."

Bobby smiled. "That's exactly what I wanted to hear. I love working in the dark and with like-minded professionals. Thank you. The computer and the office next to mine are all yours. Let me know if you need anything. We have a break room stocked with various beverages and treats. Help yourself."

Wanda stepped into the adjoining office, opened her case, removed the equipment, connected it to the laptop, and began the quest to find answers to Bobby's questions.

DeLorean hung up the phone and sat back in the chair. He felt mounting pressure to find Albright's documents and the possibility that Major Brooks was alive and in the DC area. He took another look at the photo and zoomed in, but the image pixelated, and he could not establish a positive ID. A few minutes later Kuka called and informed him she returned to the Finnish Embassy hoping to secure sources who had access to the traffic camera system. This was the second time in a month she reached out to her covert political contacts for assistance. He was happy hearing her upbeat voice; her passion was restored. He needed a break, so he stepped out of his office to visit with his team to see if anything surfaced about Albright. After 15 minutes, he returned to his office with the same answer…nothing. The stretch helped the feeling return to his legs. He sat and picked up the cell phone. Browsed his contact list and pressed the 'call' button. After three rings, the party answered.

"Hey D-Meister, what's up with you?"

DeLorean always smiled when called that nickname. One of Bobby's Delta commanders had given it because he helped the D-Boys (Delta) and it associated him with mission support. "I need a favor."

"Wow! Talk about a field flashback! You only call when you need something. You sound like my kids. What's up?"

"I need you to run a tag. It seems we may have a covert soft target assassination attempt and I need to keep this below the radar."

"Really? Anyone, I know?"

"Possibly, but I cannot say anything now."

His voice was serious. "Ok, what's the tag and state?"

DeLorean provided the information and was told to sit tight for a minute.

"Where did you see the vehicle with this number?"

"Near Arlington, why?"

"It's a spook. No tags. No names. Nothing on any system! My guess CIA because NSA doesn't get their hands dirty. If they had weapons, they could be contractors or Spec-Ops."

"They had military-grade suppressed small arms."

"Then it's serious business, my friend. I would immediately step away. Curiosity has killed more than one cat."

DeLorean lowered his head. "Thank you. I appreciate your help. If I get a positive ID on the subject, I'll let you know. Thanks again." He disconnected and sat back. This was an unexpected twist. It seems the kill team assumed it was a soft target. They were wrong; whoever the target was, they were a high-profile critical element with extensive evasive techniques. Not a run-of-the-mill person. This added to the intrigue of what happened and why.

HUDDLE - Chapter 6

The first day back on the 12th was better than expected. Everyone was immediately onboard and asked no questions outside of the related topics, each focused on their assignments with no reservations. As Bobby drove, he called Marty. "How was your day?"

"It was routine. Nothing has changed except for some additional information. Are we getting together later to review my notes?"

"Yes. Let's meet at 1900 hours and I'll bring the pizza. Does that sound good to you?"

"I'm starving. Can we make it 1800?"

"Sure. Not a problem. Thanks, and I'll see you in about 45 minutes."

DeLorean was still sitting at his desk, reviewing the incident from every news agency available. Only one photo showed the alleged victim. Kuka had texted him that some of her contacts/investigators had already come up with nothing. DeLorean had shared his discovery earlier that this was covert. Regardless, they would let nothing stop them from pursuing every source possible. The resemblance of the man to Major Brooks kept DeLorean engaged. He would not stop until a positive or negative ID was established.

Bobby was right on time with the pizza. Marty opened the door, and Bobby walked in and placed the pizza on the dining room table.

"That smells great! Where did you get it?"

"Yourmommaknows!"

Marty looked confused. "What?"

"Yourmommaknows Pizza."

"What the heck is that? Who is that?"

Bobby laughed. Marty stared at him, which made him laugh harder. Then Marty laughed, and they continued until each started crying.

After a few minutes, Bobby composed himself. "It's a wordplay I heard one day and now I always use it. It makes me laugh."

Marty rolled her eyes. "You think?"

"I haven't laughed that hard for years. Thanks, Marty. Your expression killed me. I started laughing and couldn't stop. Oh man, that was fun."

"So, what was it you said?"

"I'll break it down for you. Your. Momma. Knows. Pizza."

Marty shook her head. "Really? That sounds a lot like an actual pizza company."

"It's ok. I'm not stealing a copyright. I am having fun. Let's eat. I don't want you to get hangry."

Marty nodded. "Yes. I am starving and we don't like hangry."

Bobby opened the box and motioned for Marty to get a piece of pizza. Once she placed the pizza on the plate, she stopped. Her expression was blank.

Bobby immediately noticed the change in her demeanor. "Marty. Marty. Are you ok?"

She slowly turned toward Bobby. "I think I just experienced an episode of PTSD."

"Why? What happened?"

"I had a flashback. We were at your house eating pizza, then I remembered the men on the front lawn and me running away as fast as I could. Then I heard your voice and ran."

"I'm sorry you relived that nightmare. Breathe."

"Ok. I hope I'm not going crazy. How often do these episodes happen?"

Bobby sighed. "Maybe once, maybe the rest of our life. Everyone reacts differently to stress and life-threatening situations. Some of my buddies are unfazed from combat, while others need meds, dogs, and therapy to sleep. The best thing is to change your train of thought if you can. Go to a happy place. Think of something happy. Like me!"

Marty groaned. "You are such a narcissist!"

Bobby laughed. "And a crazy one at that!"

Marty smiled. "Regardless, you are always here for me, and I thank you for helping me. Now I need to eat before I go to an unhappy place...hanger."

She paused while Bobby prayed before they ate. She knew his routine.

They ate in silence until Bobby finished. "I made it through my first day."

Marty raised an eyebrow. "Did you expect anything less?"

"No, but it went better than I could have imagined."

Marty smiled. "That's great!"

Bobby nodded. "How was your day?"

Marty frowned. "It wasn't fun. I was alone and missed your company."

"I'm sorry. Hang in there! We all have a mission to do, and we're doing everything possible to protect Doctor Albright and his documents."

It was at that point that Marty stopped, looked up, and said, "I notice something interesting today."

"What was it?"

"Hidden in plain sight."

Bobby was puzzled. "Hidden in plain sight? Am I missing something?"

Marty shrugged her shoulders. "It's probably nothing, but as I continue the review of each page, something is pulling on my psyche. I'm seeing something materialize that is beyond the documents, going beyond the superficial evidence of recorded historical events."

Bobby turned his palms up to prompt her to continue speaking.

"It's as if there's a theme in each story that hints of other information. It goes beyond the written archives. My gut keeps telling me there is something bigger than the obvious."

"Ok. What is your gut feeling?"

"Earlier, I wrote one word for each topic that reminded me of the content. Then it hit me! There is another perspective. That something bigger than the obvious gut feeling came true as I realized we need to consider more than the face value of the documents."

Bobby was engaged. "What perspective?"

"Today, my review manifested a distinct consideration while writing the summative. There is a connection between today's words and those of past reviews; a correlation that jumped off the pages. For the first time, I wasn't reading a dossier. I wasn't reading a reflection of specific historical events." Bobby shifted in the chair. "I was reading a review of hidden missions that had been purposely hidden within the topic content."

Bobby raised his eyebrows. "Marty, everything is planned. I'm missing something. What exactly are you saying? What do you mean?"

Marty leaned in toward Bobby. "It's not a historical dossier as we originally believed. This may sound crazy, and I don't know how to say it, so I'm going to say it straight out. These papers are documentation of a manifesto."

Bobby was shocked. "How is that possible? Albright has been straight up with us. From day one. His information is methodical."

Marty smiled. "Exactly! Methodical and purposeful, but remember your words, 'Hidden in plain sight.' I'm not saying Albright is part of a grand scheme, but as we review events that outline and portray history, another perspective must be considered. I ventured outside the box. I'm seeing everything from a new perspective that shows the papers could be tools to disguise the truth and lead us away from the facts."

Bobby interrupted. "The facts are right in front of us."

Marty put her hand in front of his face. "Listen carefully. Everything revolves around the White House and the person seated behind the *Resolute Desk*. It's about the

Presidents and events that happened during their administrations. Events that were planned. Orchestrated!"

Bobby was silent as he concentrated on her words. He was breaking them down into the possibilities of what could and could not be true.

"Review my notes. When you read the abbreviated notations, you will see it too."

"Do you know how incredible and crazy this sounds?"

Marty smiled. "Yes. This is exactly why I'm on this like white on rice."

Bobby was surprised. She joked during a revelation of this magnitude. "So, you are telling me every President of the United States, beginning with FDR, has colluded in questionable activities and/or abuses of power while seated?"

Marty smiled. "That's not exactly what I am saying! However, there are two emerging patterns! Either this is the biggest conspiracy in history, or these men have been used as puppets to engage in activities ordered by a puppet master...a political puppeteer!"

Bobby was astounded. "That sounds so ridiculous it could be true! Hidden in plain sight. I cannot believe these words may come to fruition in this arena. If orders are coming from outside the White House, there must be a manifesto. If there is a manifesto who wrote it and where is it? Albright's documents are not a manifesto. They are evidence of elements and incidents within a manifesto that happened, who was involved, and when they happened. Is there a hidden agenda to take control of the presidency? The world?"

Marty sat quietly, trying to fathom what her perspective manifested. "Could this be what Dr. Albright meant about the last days, the hidden message, or am I looking too deep?"

Bobby continued. "Right now, I don't know. I found it intriguing that Albright had copies of Huxley's, *Brave New World*, which outlines a dystopian society, and Orwell's *1984*. Coincidence or possible road maps?"

"The odds of president after president creating an agenda that aligned with the previous administration is possible, but holding each administration hostage by powerful decades-long, growing cabal is possible, but believable. This would be the largest orchestrated extortion operation in history."

Bobby was focused. "Of all the conspiracy theories I have heard and considered, I believe this is possible and could usher in a *New World Order* overseen by a secret power of elite individuals with enough money and influence to create a global agenda."

Marty chimed in. "An organization that would eventually replace every political office of the world and result in an authoritarian one-world government. An all-encompassing propaganda-driven ideology that overthrows all governments. The culmination of dictating several presidents and contemporary figures into pawns as the plans of orchestrating significant political and financial events cause systemic crises that embrace controversial policies at every national and international level leading to world domination."

Marty was giddy. "I know how they will do it."

Bobby motioned her to proceed as though he were holding the door open.

"They use fear motivating tactics. History shows that political factions and ideological dictators who use fear motivating tactics can persuade people to sacrifice food, property, and freedom."

Bobby shook his head in disbelief, knowing she was right. "Let's also consider the changes in American culture. People are afraid and are actively preparing for apocalyptic scenarios. Shelters, purified water, stockpiles of food, and fuel. Political scientists are concerned that mass hysteria over famine and fuel could have devastating effects on American political life, ranging from escalating lone-wolf terrorism to a rise to power from authoritarians or ultranationalist demagogues."

Marty sat back. "This is deep, Bobby. I think we need to investigate this from a new perspective."

Bobby nodded. "I have not felt this way for years, but I am scared. If you are right. Whoever is behind this has the power and influence to skew the truth and control world leaders, the banks, the media, communications, and electrical grids. We already know they are using education to indoctrinate and control future generations. The thing tugging at my thoughts is, if true, what do they want to accomplish?"

ARISTOCRACY OR ANARCHY? - Chapter 7

The Aristocrat walked into the office. As he strolled toward the desk, he was basking in opulence. Surrounded by symbols of wealth that filled the room was a diverse collection of history ranging from paintings, statues, and artifacts that rivaled the *Smithsonian*. He never failed to savor the feeling of distinction when he walked the 50 feet from the door to his desk; his office was more than a token of authority, it was a symbol of aristocracy. The room, filled with representations of his influence to get what he wanted, fueled his insatiable ego, which made him the epitome of narcissism. His thirst for more possessions, power, and control consumed his maniacal passion and twisted psyche. At this point in life, he had sculpted a personal culture few would ever experience and most envied. He stood behind the exquisite leather chair and placed his hands on the headrest. His gaze scanned the room one last time before sitting.

He felt emboldened.

Before him was a folder with the bold red inscription, "*Top Secret UMBRA.*" A sinister grin formed on his face. His vast resources of wealth and political contacts provided boundless opportunities to get anything and everything desired. He slowly opened the dossier and read in the solitude of a Saturday evening.

Bobby was relaxing on the couch, watching the evening news. The headline was about how a group of German citizens, extremists believed to be *Reich Citizens* who subscribed to the *QAnon* ideology, were arrested.

Hundreds of police and Spec-Op military members were dispatched to execute arrests and search warrants throughout Germany. The arrests of perpetrators included a member of the most recognized families in Germany. Former Spec-Op military leaders and enlisted members were gathered and arrested. Included were a retired judge and former lawmaker. These professionals did not fit the typical profile of young uneducated people indoctrinated to evolve from protesters to terrorists. These were members with extensive military and political experience on the mission to overthrow the current German government and install new leadership that aligned with the *QAnon* and *Reich Citizen* philosophies. Bobby's concentration was interrupted by a knock on the door. He arose, walked to the door, and peeked through the peephole. Then yelled. "We don't want any! I already gave at the office." He quickly opened the door as Marty rushed in. "So much for not drawing attention to ourselves, Einstein!"

Bobby grimaced. "Oops! Sorry about that lady. I guess our ruse has been compromised. They will surely find us now!" Bobby casually walked to the couch and sat. "Fortunately, I have been keeping tabs on the number of guests sharing this floor. It's practically vacant. Therefore, we remain hidden in plain sight!"

Marty grinned. "You really like that statement, don't you? What is your infatuation with it?"

Bobby smirked. "Infatuation? Really? You are in the presence of genius, and you mock me with your paltry attempts to belittle me? Away with you knave!"

Marty shook her head. "Knave? Now you are a king who looks down on me?"

"Yes! It's good to be king! Correction! It's great to be king!"

"You mean it's great to be insane, don't you? What the heck did you eat or drink today?"

Bobby laughed. "Nothing! I'm messing with you. I was watching the news about some extremists in Germany who want to overthrow the current government. It was reported they subscribe to the *QAnon* and *Reich Citizen* philosophies."

Marty quickly glanced at Bobby. "*QAnon*? I've heard of it, but I'm not sure what it is."

"It allegedly began by an American far-right political group in 2017 based on a conspiracy theory."

Marty shook her head. "Why am I not surprised you know that?"

"Hold on. There is more. Their philosophy revolves around fabricated claims made by anonymous individuals which make it anonymously anonymous."

Marty gave a pitiful grin as Bobby smiled and continued.

"These anonymous individuals are identified as 'Q.' Sounds like something you would find in a *James Bond* novel. Anyway, the lies, they call fact, have been relayed, developed, embellished, and supplemented throughout their communities by influencers associated with the movement. The core conspiracy theory is that a cabal of violent, political, Satanic, cannibalistic, antisemitic, child sexual abusers who operate a global sex trafficking ring that conspired against former U.S. Presidents and the Jews. Did I miss any undesirable faction of the community?"

Marty was astonished. "Are you serious? How can this be possible, and nothing is being done about it?"

Bobby nodded. "Politics and perversion are great bed buddies... pun intended. By the way, did you notice the correlation between your out-of-the-box perspective and the philosophy of these Germans regarding a New World Order?"

Marty froze. "No, but I see it now. This is getting crazy. What's next?"

"My consideration? Let's see if Albright knows anything about these people and if his documents outline a bigger situation."

Marty looked up into Bobby's eyes. "Are you serious? What if he gets upset knowing we discovered something never expected? What if we open *Pandora's Box?*"

Bobby winked. "Then we have a *Pandora's Box* problem. I believe Albright expects us to find the hidden agenda. Why would he risk the chance of us discovering something he never intended to expose? Let's change the subject and take a break from the drama. We can resume this Monday. Sit down and watch some television with me."

Marty sat as Bobby took the remote and began channel surfing. Twenty minutes later, they agreed to watch a classic movie.

He closed the dossier, reached across the desk, and removed a Cuban cigar from the cedar humidor. He cut the tip, placed the cigar in his mouth, and applied fire with a torch lighter. After several slow, deep draws, he looked at the tip to ensure the burn was even. He sat back. The cigar provided the subtle relaxation needed to suppress his stress as he reflected on hate; the irony of being too powerful. He was incensed and wanted these people dead. There would be no other means to satisfy his disdain for them. They were standing between him and his reservation with destiny. They were expendable and he would ensure they disappeared without a trace. No one, not one person, would impede his mission, his goals, and his dreams. Others had tried to stop him before, and they all shared the same fate of dying from lead poisoning; a dose of 9mm lead to the base of the skull. He would do whatever was necessary to bring his destiny to fruition.

The world did not know him, but soon everyone would know his name.

He would overthrow every political socialist, communist, and capitalist; he would publicly strip them of everything they had. His quest was fueled by the thirst to see them begging and crawling before him, acknowledging he was superior in every manner and having them beg for his mercy. The sarcastic grin reappeared. His solution for their cowardly humility and groveling would be a public execution. He hated anyone who was not ready to face death. The only solution was to rid society of these weak-minded people with the sword. The graphic display of a sword impaling or decapitating a person spoke volumes. The expression on their faces as the sword went completely through their bodies was a statement of power. He would control life and death. This would be his time to show his strength and resolve while subjecting everyone to compliance using fear; nobody would challenge him. He picked up the phone and dialed.

Two rings later, the call was answered. "I take it you got the papers?"

The Aristocrat smiled. "Yes. Well done, my friend. I appreciate your contribution to the mission."

"My pleasure. Have a wonderful day. We will be in touch. Goodbye." With that, he placed the receiver back into the cradle, turned his chair to the window, and watched the bird float gracefully in a crystal-clear blue sky.

PERKS AND QUIRKS - Chapter 8

The Aristocrat scheduled the meeting with his team of specialists. Men and women representing some of the best operators in the world. His team resembled a group of *French Foreign Legionaries* comprising a cross-section of various races and nationalities, working in unison for a collective mission and purpose. The Aristocrat asked the operators to meet at the training grounds in the middle of the 40-acre establishment. This was the perfect location for covert operations, weapons training, evasive driving techniques, close-quarter battle, improvised explosive devices, and the development of other terminal skills and scenarios. It was just before sunset as the members mustered outside the armory. The Aristocrat arrived in his custom *Land Rover* and walked before the members. He spoke. "Thank you for meeting me here on such short notice. I have some important information to share with you that will show how much I value each of you and the integrity you bring to our organization. I cannot share my gratitude in mere words. I thank everyone for your dedication and devotion to making this company the iconic example of who specialized operators are and what they are expected to do without hesitation or failure. Several news agencies have recognized our efforts as the benchmark of professional contract military services, of which you have set the bar so high it is out of reach for anyone else."

He applauded the members as he paced before them. They joined him with cheering. After a minute, he gestured for quiet, then spoke. "Before I continue, I want to recognize three of your peers. I want you to understand my devotion to each of you and how the completion of every mission is critical." He applauded again while nodding his head toward the three members. He motioned for them to join him. As they walked toward him, he reminded everyone of the critical importance that every mission is completed properly; if not, the team and mission would be compromised. Any failure could expose the operations, the operators, and the location of the business, and endanger everyone, including their families. The operators stood alongside him in front of their comrades.

He stepped before each man and shook their hands, then hugged them. "Before you are three of your brothers. These men understand the importance of engaging the target after properly assessing the situation and doing what was necessary to fulfill the task; even if it requires making split-second decisions that may not be embraced by society. We have a mission to do, and we will do whatever is required to successfully complete it."

The tone of his voice and expression changed. "Unfortunately, these men failed to successfully complete their last mission. They failed, and failure is not part of our operations. Look at them!" As he pointed toward the three men, and as if on cue, each man's head snapped back as the crack of a bullet traveling faster than 1,100 feet per second broke the sound barrier with the simultaneous impact of 7.62 full metal jacketed rounds entering their foreheads and making gaping exit wounds while spewing blood and gray matter behind them.

The men were dead on their feet as their lifeless bodies fell next to each other.

No one saw the three snipers located two hundred yards behind the group who used suppressed *SIG 716 DMR semiautomatic sniper rifles*, but the evidence of their presence was immediately realized. They stood in silence, but their expressions assured the Aristocrat's message was clearly understood as he walked toward their bodies.

He stood over them and pointed down while gazing into the eyes of the crowd. "These individuals failed me, they failed you, and they failed our illustrious institution. This is the price for failure! Anyone who fails will incur this payment. Let me reiterate, no one fails me or my organization. If they do, they become a vivid reminder of the consequences for others to see! When you fall short, you will fall before me!" His callous statement shocked the people. Most had seen and experienced the horrors of war, but he was beyond civility as he mocked their deaths. "Look at their contorted faces. This is an example of the damage a 7.62 bullet does when impacting the dense bone of the frontal skull and passing through the cerebral cortex and exiting with half the brain tissue. Their skulls are no longer intact... that's why their faces look like discarded Halloween masks tossed to the ground."

Everyone stood in silence, staring at the Aristocrat, and occasionally looking at the contorted faces of their former teammates. The Aristocrat yelled. "In the training building are three body bags, latex gloves, and three shovels. Go get them, put this garbage in the bags, drive to the farthest northern point of the property, and bury them in the landfill. That is a fitting burial for failures such as these. Questions?" The air was silent. "Good! Then get to work. Report back at 0600 for PT and your bonus checks."

The commander stepped forward. "Bonus checks?"

"Yes. The wages of these three failures will be distributed equally to the professionals who are standing before me. Also, you will have three replacements report to you in the morning. Be sure you onboard them immediately. No background check is needed. They proved themselves worthy today." He walked to his *Land Rover* and drove off. The commander looked at the group. "You heard him. Let's get this done."

William Martin appreciated the access he had to all classified archives. His quest to find the reason Albright met with Churchill continued each day after he completed the field report reviews. Frequently, he thought he came close to discovering the reason for their meeting, but fell short of finding concrete evidence. Today seemed no different. Before resuming the Albright endeavor, he would go to the

Tea House Theatre and order fish and chips; seems he had a strange craving for that dish after a recent encounter and introduction. Two hours later, with a full stomach, he was gleaning more of Churchill's documents. After reviewing the first stack of pages, he picked up the second. Interestingly, the first page was a photo of President Woodrow Wilson and Winston Churchill. This was an unexpected find because Wilson was president before Churchill was Prime Minister. Why would these two men be together when their positions of responsibility and authority occurred in different decades? William was perplexed as the intrigue of his investigation expanded. He had to find out when and where this photograph was taken.

Fortunately, he had the internet. He wouldn't need the secret vault of MI6 files. All he needed was to access the online *Woodrow Wilson Presidential Library,* where he would peruse the website and, if necessary, contact the staff and request they identify the location of Wilson and Churchill. This was the easiest venture while vetting the archives for the Albright-Churchill meeting. After 30 minutes of navigating the website, he found nothing that would connect the dots. He called the library and requested information about the photograph. They requested a copy, which he promptly emailed. Now he had to wait. He sat and relaxed.

He felt confident and believed this would help him.

At this point in his investigation, he hoped the photo would help him discover how Albright fit into the Churchill equation. He took a trip to the loo and returned a few minutes later. He sat and checked his email, hoping for good news, and was pleased to see the librarian had responded. The correspondence was succinct and referred him to review the copy-and-paste response, which was fine. He printed the content and began his first review. Five minutes later, he sat back, recapping what he read. He then put the papers in order and read them again. This time with the pen and highlighter in hand to identify key points. In his position, details were something that could never be taken for granted; he learned the importance of critical review. He discovered that political bantering has been around for many years. This article showed the arrogance of American leaders encouraged the publishing of unequally favorable responses to any criticism foreign dignitaries published regarding the performance of American presidents.

Nothing was sacred to the Americans…not even other Americans!

This was a learning experience for him. Churchill's notoriety during World War II highlighted his legacy while other endeavors sat in the shadows. It was revealed these men had met at the *League of Nations* meeting in Paris where Wilson outlined his famous ill-gotten *Fourteen Points*. Churchill's critique, political bantering, noted Wilson was attempting to create world democracy in his image…the democracy of a *New World Order*.

President Wilson didn't mince words in his responses; he went straight for the *Jugular Vein* of cliquish and self-interested governments. Wilson emphasized America was the only nation dedicated to the interests of mankind as other nations fell short. He heralded the theme, "No more war, something for our own country to bring Americans home safely." He added America desired no conquest and no dominion with no expectations of material compensation for the sacrifices, but touted a *New World Order (NWO)*. Wilson's introduction of NWO concluded with the same theme he used in the introduction that Americans are the champions of humanity. Churchill saw the possibilities of Wilson's NWO vision but realistically looked at the obstacles that impeded Wilson's dream. Churchill believed it was doomed to failure. Martin realized this was a no-holds-barred exchange.

Unfortunately, the information failed to mention Albright. There was one thing he would further investigate was Wilson's idea of a *New World Order*; maybe this approach would reveal an Albright and Churchill connection. *New World Order* was outside of any common vernacular for that time, but Wilson's vision introduced the world to a new perspective on solving problems. William began an Internet search for *New World Order* topics and was overwhelmed by the results. He never expected to see how many Christians, atheists, radical groups, and even H. G. Wells shared common perspectives on President Wilson's *New World Order*. He read some responses but shrugged them off as a waste of time; however, his question remained, "Where is Albright, and could the *New World Order* ideals connect him to Churchill? Was there a correlation?"

UNEXPECTED HISTORY - Chapter 9

    Monday morning came too soon. Bobby was up early performing his calisthenics while watching the sports news; his primary interest outside of protecting Albright and the documents. After concluding his workout, he sat and switched to the news. His timing was perfect as the headlines shared more details regarding the attempted coup d'état from extremist German factions. German Prosecutors reiterated the arrests of several nationals and one Russian who subscribed to the goal of overthrowing what they called "the illegitimate, deep-state German democratic constitutional government" by forcible elimination was the tip of the iceberg. The prosecutor continued detailing the largest counter-terrorism operation in the country's history. Special notice was given regarding the continued investigation of other suspects, both in and out of Germany. The prosecutor concluded by saying the terrorists were inspired by several conspiracy myths and ideologies specific to *Reichsbürger* and *QAnon*; similar to the American beliefs of the sovereign-citizen movement and the opposing philosophical indoctrination of a *New World Order*. Bobby made several mental notes about the German situation. This added more intrigue to Albright's words and experiences as he prepared to share his discoveries with Albright. He turned off the television and headed to the shower.

    Before reporting to the office, Bobby kept his promise to meet Marty at the *Smithsonian* so they could talk with Albright and, if possible, share the political issues occurring in Germany. At exactly 0700, Marty met Bobby in the parking area. They walked through their designated safe area. Bobby updated Marty on the German issues and shared some information about player changes and trades with the Packers, specifically the quarterback position. As they entered the main hall, they heard Dr. Martinez speaking. The expanse of the halls provided unobstructed eavesdropping on any conversation. Bobby glanced at Marty as they approached her office. Just before knocking, Bobby was surprised. "Martinez! What are you doing here?"

The sergeant looked back with equal astonishment. By that time Marty was peeking around Bobby to see who he was speaking with.

"I came to see my mom."

Bobby and Marty exclaimed together. "Your mom!"

"Yes, my mom."

Dr. Martinez stepped forward. "Before anyone thinks or says anything, let me explain."

Everyone was already thinking about the moment and exchanged glances in silence.

"As you might have already guessed, Sergeant Martinez is my son. I was unaware he was assigned to you in combat and network security."

Bobby's expression was blank. "Martinez, you know the protocol for leaking classified information, especially in our unit. I could bring you up on treason if you have shared anything with your mother outside of our operational security."

The office went silent, then quickly directed their attention to the hall as they heard. "I told her. I felt it was best to bring her up to speed if this ever happened."

Everyone quickly directed their attention to the voice in the hallway.

Albright stood behind them. "This was my call."

Bobby relaxed. "That changes everything! I'm sorry for jumping to conclusions, Martinez. I mean Dr. and Sergeant Martinez."

Bobby's communication fumble lightened the air as the tension eased.

Marty raised her hands. "Ok. Everyone needs to relax! This was unexpected, but it has not impacted our mission or integrity. However, unexpected is a gross understatement regarding what I witnessed...a family reunion of sorts."

Dr. Albright nodded. "Marty is right. This does not compromise the mission and yes, 'unexpected' falls short of detailing the surprise we all experienced. Is everyone well?"

Everyone nodded in agreement. Sergeant Martinez spoke. "Why wasn't I informed of these issues and unknown connections?"

Bobby thought there was more to this situation than what was being said and seen. "What do you mean? What unknown connections? That's plural. Is there more to this than we are being told?"

Albright cleared his throat. "You have a keen sense of observation. Let's step back and allow me to fill in some additional blanks."

Again, everyone exchanged glances in silence.

"Please allow me to make proper introductions. First, this is my daughter, Dr. Martinez."

Marty interrupted. "What? That makes Sergeant Martinez your grandson. I didn't see this coming."

"Yes. Seems we occasionally have a family gathering in the basement."

Marty was beside herself, and Bobby wasn't far behind. Marty asked, "So, how is this possible?"

For the next ten minutes, Albright told them about the events that took place when he was assigned to Mexico City. The meeting, the relationship, the marriage, the birth, and the death. He stopped several times to compose himself because of the emotionally charged conversation that opened deep, painful secrets and memories. By the time he finished, everyone had shed tears.

Marty was the first to respond. "I cannot fathom the emotional roller coaster of pain and frustration you experienced during that time. The distance between you both. The birth, and the moment she was gone. I'm so sorry."

Bobby immediately joined in. "I share Marty's words. I'm sorry you had to bring this to the table today."

Albright smiled. "Believe it or not, the pain of sharing also produces healing as I reminisced about the moments we shared. I'm glad I gave you all a peek into the private life of the man few people have ever known. Until today, I put everything in the recesses of my mind into a black box. Now, I feel some of the weight lifted from my heart."

Everyone stood in silence, then began hugging each other. Afterward, Albright looked at Bobby. "What brought you here this morning?"

Bobby smiled. "I wanted to talk to you about the arrests in Germany. Have you heard about them?"

"No, but we don't need to be preoccupied with *Reichsbürger* and *QAnon* right now. Let's try to meet up later this week. How about Wednesday morning?"

Bobby nodded. "That's fine with me. Just let me know what time. With that, I'll head back to the office." As Bobby turned to walk away, he spoke to Martinez. "I'll see you at the office. Remember, none of this happened. Marty, let's review your notes tonight."

"Of course. I'll need someone to open the vault."

Dr. Martinez motioned she would open the vault.

Sergeant Martinez gave a visual thumbs-up cue to Bobby that he would meet him at the office.

"See you all later." With that, Bobby walked away as Marty turned toward the vault and Dr. Martinez hugged her son, then headed to the vault. Dr. Albright patted Sergeant Martinez on the back, then hugged him. Albright walked toward his office as Sergeant Martinez tried to close the gap between him and Bobby.

DID HE NOTICE? - Chapter 10

Bobby and Sergeant Martinez arrived on the 12th floor at 0900. Traffic from downtown DC to Rockville was horrible; unfortunately, that was the status quo for driving, but it provided each ample time to digest the events of an impromptu family reunion at the *Smithsonian*. He stopped at each member's office and touched bases to get updates on their activities, and if any security issues were discovered, that needed closer attention. Everyone was good, so he returned to his office. He noticed some of Chang's remnants on the desk and he presumed more of his property was in the drawers. It was time to clean up. He picked up the trash can and placed it next to the desk as he sat. He carefully emptied each drawer and set some items aside on the desk for a more detailed examination to see what trash was and what could be saved for Chang's family. He finally made it to the last drawer...the large right-side drawer.

He began emptying the contents and discovered an unopened, thin box addressed to him. After last week's attempted assassination, he cautiously evaluated the package, and after a minute, he was convinced it was too thin to be anything outside of a chemical or powder. He went to the armory and got a pair of latex gloves, then carefully opened the package and removed its contents. There was one black-and-white photo and a sales receipt. In all the excitement, he had forgotten about this order before disappearing into thin air. He remembered having a conversation with Chang about the man in the photograph. It was as though it was yesterday when he shared the history of Finnish Soldier Lauri Allan Törni (aka Green Beret Larry Alan Thorne), a man driven by the lust of battle and hate for his enemy. Bobby felt the pain when Chang was gone. He didn't die a soldier's death in the heat of battle. Chang died by his hand by his own decision, unlike the ultimate soldier Larry Alan Thorne, who was on a recon mission in Vietnam. Why would Chang keep my package in his drawer? That didn't make sense since it was known I was dead. Why would Chang, an accused double agent, or a spy for China, keep a possession belonging to a dead man? It doesn't make sense. It was kept for a reason. What was Chang thinking?

Some things don't make sense.

He looked at the black-and-white photograph of decorated Green Beret Larry Alan Thorne. Bobby felt the battle growing in his mind. Two things didn't register. First, his gut told him something wasn't right about Chang's incident and his gut was never wrong. Second, he continued to think about this situation as he examined the *Post-Its*, notes, notepads, pencils, and the book he held in his hand. He turned it over to read the cover, *Sun Tzu–The Art of War*. This was curious. He opened the book to a page marked with a paper clip. There was a highlighted sentence, "*Keep your friends close and your enemies closer.*" This added to his suspicions that something was not right about Chang's incident. The second concern came to mind. "Why would Albright say he hadn't heard about the German incidents and arrests, then specifically identify the perpetrators? His identification of the radical groups after claiming no knowledge of the incident was puzzling." He set the book aside and continued organizing the office while thinking about these two issues. Thirty minutes later, Bobby still didn't know why Chang killed himself or why Albright denied knowing about the German issue. Maybe Albright misunderstood me or wasn't aware of my question. Nothing about these two issues could be ignored. Bobby continued focusing his attention on finding the facts about Chang and Albright. He would also schedule a meeting with Martinez to review Chang's activities before his death, then schedule another meeting with Albright for next Wednesday to clarify some questions.

The Aristocrat sat at his desk. The gold-plated telephone receiver was pressed against his ear as he screamed into the microphone. This was his signature manner of making his point known and understood to whoever was listening as he reiterated, "I don't care who is involved with us. I did what I had to do. Those men failed us. I made an indelible reminder of what happens when anyone in this organization fails. I don't care about witnesses. No one will say anything for fear of reaping the same repercussion. They are weak. They know nothing about leadership, about accountability. Compared to me, they are a group of hens hiding from a fox! We have made sacrifices and we will make more. They are misguided and disconnected, while I am not altruistic. I am narcissistic.

I am the Cabal.

No one is as powerful as me in this organization. No one has the fortitude to do the ugly things necessary to seize control and no one ever will. This is my destiny, my purpose, and my moment! Tell them what I said and if they don't like it, too bad!" He slammed the receiver down and sat back in the chair. His lips were tense and the furrow between his eyes was deep with frustration. Sweat formed on his forehead. He hated inept people. He hated hesitation. There was no time to banter about the disposal of the three losers. He knew hesitation was a toxic mental lapse of action for the weak. He was aggressive and his mantra for caution was, *"He who hesitates loses."* He took some deep breaths and exhaled slowly. He had the gut feeling someone was monitoring him. Unfortunately, he didn't know if it was from within or outside of the organization. He knew the killing of the three failures could interfere with his goals, but he took the chance and made an example of them. Failure was never an option and anything of this magnitude could never be hidden in plain sight. Whoever was monitoring his operations was not a field operator fighting half a world away. He believed domestic operators from within his organization could be aligning with the enemy in a rogue Psy-Op-Controlled counter-operation designed to destroy his dreams of total domination; this was larger than anything he had faced before, and he was prepared to die if necessary. His goal was to ferret out anyone involved and control the outcome by removing all evidence of his evolving rogue network with a plan to overtake the political world! His psychological control for dominance was almost complete as the gears of his insanity slowly turned. He looked around the office. There were no windows to monitor his movement as he sat in solitude. His only friend was obscurity, which is why no one could enter or monitor his haven of power or use electronic eavesdropping equipment. This was his safe room.

BREAKFAST - Chapter 11

DeLorean and Kuka met for breakfast. She was tired. She was frustrated, and she was angry. After placing their orders, she leaned across the table and looked him directly in the eyes, asking, "Why is Albright so important?"

DeLorean paused before speaking. "It's not that Albright is important; Albright's papers are important."

"What is it about these papers? What do they contain?"

DeLorean shifted in the chair. "For several decades, Albright has allegedly documented everything he saw and heard while holding the exclusive front row confidant, attaché if I may, to several presidents of the United States."

Kuka asked. "Am I to assume these 'alleged' documents contain classified information?"

He nodded. "That is what everyone has been thinking, even if we don't know the documents actually exist."

"That's crazy! I could be on a wild goose chase for someone who may not exist. Does Albright actually exist or is he another alleged element in what I'm seeing as a waste of time? I'm not surprised the government would spend money looking for something that doesn't exist. Remember *Project Blue Book*? Nothing. Now, decades later, some conspiracy theorists are trying to rekindle the hunt for UFOs. Incredible! Maybe Albright and his 'alleged' papers were abducted by aliens."

DeLorean frowned. "This is not the conversation to bring additional speculation in, even if it is humor. Whoever ordered the search for Albright and his documents has the authority and purpose, regardless of if it's a wild goose chase or not, to give specific orders. If the documents exist and speculation of their information is correct, they would be worth their weight in gold. Imagine having privy to secrets about every president's private life, their affairs, their health issues, their competence during their administration, and their integrity. During Reagan's last year of his administration, Nancy was running the country because of his mental degradation. Then we can consider the political issues, the wars, the covert operations, and the spying on anyone and everyone in the world. The Israelis had a meltdown when they discovered the United States was spying on them. However, they quieted down when we proved they were spying on us, too. The is no trust in the world…even with our allies."

Kuka interjected. "Yes, and this reminds me of children waiting for *Santa Claus* to bring them gifts. Their minds run wild with thoughts of every gift possible. However, I'm seeing several red flags here, brother."

DeLorean shared another perspective. "I want you to consider this. Even if some of these issues are not in the documents, how do you think the world would react if our use of military equipment and personnel were tied to war crimes or endorsed and covered up the war crimes of other nations?"

> *"These revelations would encourage more hostilities and war."*

"I believe the passion to find Albright and his documents is to save face. The secrets of the United States cannot be paraded before the world; especially if they discredit or embarrass us. We would immediately become a pariah and fall from grace and align with the leadership of any third-world country. Exposing our dirty laundry of corrupt leaders, graft, thievery, adultery, murder, orchestrating wars for gain, or whatever it is, would destroy our credibility. This is the fear which motivates the search for Albright and his documents."

Kuka looked as if she was surprised. She didn't expect to hear her brother say all the details about Albright. She inquired, "How do you know about Albright?"

DeLorean looked to his left and right. "I'm the guy that put Albright on the 6th floor. I was the guy tasked with removing him from society. He was supposed to die on the sixth floor, and any knowledge of his existence and the documents would have died with him. Unfortunately, he didn't die, he escaped."

"How is it you became the guy that put Albright on some 6th floor, and what is this 6th floor you are talking about?"

DeLorean paused as the server delivered breakfast. After she left, he shared more information. "Albright stepped into a perfect storm right out of college. The timing was ideal for him because, as a young, articulate genius with a near-photographic memory, his characteristics were exactly what President Franklin Delano Roosevelt was looking for. It was during the depression that Roosevelt realized the need to have an attaché next to him, to be his legs. He wanted someone he could trust to reach out to the dignitaries of the world on his behalf; to represent him. Albright became that person when the problems with the Japanese escalated and brought us into World War II on December 7, 1941. Roosevelt had another issue too…the battles in the European theater. Hitler was insane and wanted to overthrow every country possible and his madness and military enterprise proved he could. Churchill reached out for help, but FDR needed a secure way to relay information to him. Roosevelt was afraid to use any type of correspondence, radio, or telephone because spies were everywhere. That's why the adage, '*Loose lips sink ships*' was passionately promoted. This was the culminating point for Albright's critical importance to be manifested in Roosevelt's image. Roosevelt called for a top-secret meeting with Albright that provided the expanding details of his position. His first mission would be to fly with a secure case handcuffed to his left arm to London in a modified P-51 fighter, where he would hand-deliver a message from Roosevelt to Churchill. Albright's evolutionary process of covert operations for the president had begun. No one knows if Roosevelt instructed Albright to take notes or document the events he experienced, but speculation drove the belief that Albright began documenting his activities to cover his butt in case he was to become the administration's sacrificial lamb. This speculation fueled fears that if Albright ever went rogue, his experiences and documents could be used as a tool to gain political power. It was obvious Albright knew he was in a gray area of domestic and international laws, but regardless of what it was or who it was, nobody knew for certain what was fact and what was speculation. Albright's specialized skills and services continued under the authority of many presidents. Albright became their critical diplomatic resource. His activities became so critical and secret that his identifier, codename, at the White House was *Shadow*."

All Secret Service agents knew of Shadow, but few ever met him.

"There was a select group of Secret Service agents with the clearance to meet him. He was allowed entry at a specific time and location each day. The purpose was to keep his identity hidden, and reduce the probability he would be compromised or recognized outside of the White House." DeLorean took a few bites of his food.

Kuka was amazed. "Why didn't you tell me any of this?"

DeLorean looked up. "Seriously? You expected me to reveal one of the most incredible secrets in recent history regarding the most powerful leaders of the world?

"I'm your sister. You're supposed to trust me."

DeLorean shook his head. "No way! I'm sorry, but in my business, I can trust no one."

She frowned. "I understand. I can't blame you. So, what's this 6th floor you are talking about?"

DeLorean shifted uncomfortably in his chair and cleared his throat. Kuka knew her brother was about to share something very important.

"Not long into Roosevelt's four-term in office, he died. At that point, it was realized our spy agencies had many operators in the Pacific and European theaters. We used every resource necessary, including Japanese Americans whose families were prisoners in internment camps, to get information. Imagine having to support the nation of whom you are a citizen while your family was imprisoned illegally. Fortunately, the integrity of the Japanese American people was far better than the integrity of the United States government. Post-World War II brought changes in world dominance after we used two nuclear devices on humans. Other nations wanted the same weaponry to protect their assets. The Soviet Union disconnected from the United States and began strengthening their weapons' arsenals, which included the atomic bomb which began the *Cold War* era."

"Excuse me, but is the history lesson pertinent to our conversation?"

DeLorean paused the conversation to take the last bites of his breakfast. "Yes. For you to completely understand the gravity of Albright, you need to know the backstage activities that contributed to where we are today."

Kuka sighed. "Continue."

DeLorean nodded and swallowed his last bite of pan-fried ham with eggs. "As I was saying. Using spies continued to be expected after the war because new wars were being created and we needed to know everything possible to ensure protection for our citizens while continuing world dominance; a process of human engagement that continues today. Then, as if someone had an epiphany, the question emerged. What if some of our aging former high-asset spies started talking about their experiences as their minds deteriorated with age? Several potential solutions were entertained, but only one could ensure the safety of our secrets. To remove them from the public. So, we began operation *Grandfather Clause*. The first thing was to create a secure operational location where these people could be housed until death."

Kuka exclaimed. "What? Death?"

"Yes. It was determined our aging spies had to be segregated from society in case they suffered any cognitive issues and started spewing out top-secret information."

Kuka exclaimed, "That's ghastly!"

"The decision was made that everyone fitting a certain category was removed and destined for death to protect the secrets."

Kuka rolled her eyes. "You better hope you're not in that category of operations, because that gives insight into what awaits you...your final destination! How did you get these people out of circulation without their families knowing? I can't imagine having someone at Thanksgiving dinner one day and then disappear the next."

"You are correct. We took every consideration to remove these people and converted a vacant, dilapidated building in the middle of commerce into our safe location."

"You mean their final destination, don't you?"

DeLorean did not expect pushback from his sister. She was a professional who normally disconnected her emotions from this mission. "Regardless of what you think. The 6th floor was home to our special operators. Hidden in plain sight doesn't raise any red flags, as you said."

Kuka shook her head. "That's horrible! How many people are lying in bed destined to die?"

"That doesn't concern you. What matters is the protection of our nation's assets. We created scenarios that were presented and accepted by their family members as accidents or unexpected disappearances, you know, a *Silver Alert*. Each person was put into a drug-induced coma until they died. Then we would notify the family that their loved one's remains had been found but required a closed casket. This would allow them to grieve and bring closure to their loss."

Kuka stared into her brother's eyes. "That is the most callous form of reward for dedication and services I have ever heard! It reminds me of someone taking their dog to the vet to be euthanized after it became too old. Unbelievable how this could be approved!"

DeLorean sighed. "You don't have to worry about that now. After I brought Albright to the 6th floor, I was promoted and moved to my current assignment. The decision was made to have me continue seeking former operatives who could jeopardize security. My replacement, Major Robert Brooks, did not know of my activities. He was given security of the building and network. Everything was going well until our illustrious enigma, Dr. Anderson Albright, disappeared into thin air. Unfortunately, after the deaths of Brooks and Bell, word got out about the purpose of the 6th-floor operations and the negative exposure immediately led to the termination of the program and several careers. Seems the political pundits who orchestrated and endorsed the program covered their butts by throwing several military and civilian members under the bus."

"Program? Is that what you called kidnapping and murder?"

"Don't get sanctimonious on me! It seems you have forgotten the blood on your hands."

Kuka rolled her eyes. "So, what happened to Albright?"

"During his stay on the 6th floor, we assume he communicated with at least one nurse, Marty, to orchestrate an escape. It is speculated his story was later shared with Major Brooks."

"How could you possibly know that?"

"Bell and Brooks took a trip together a few weeks before Albright's disappearance."

Kuka raised her eyebrows. "They took a trip together, which makes them culpable?"

"Not that they took a trip together. The trip they took ended up at the home of Anderson Albright in Norwalk, Iowa. Something we did not know and are now routinely surveilling. We discovered, using a spy satellite, they took a large box with them. We do not know the contents of the box, but assumed it was something important. When they returned to Rockville, we were tailing them and saw the box taken into the Major's house. We considered breaching the location when he was working, but took a less invasive approach and planted eavesdropping devices on the windows so we could monitor and record all their conversations. Bell and Brooks met each day after work for several hours."

"Why did they meet?"

DeLorean smiled. "They were reviewing documents that outlined meetings with FDR, General Groves, Winston Churchill, and J. Robert Oppenheimer."

Kuka's face went blank.

"Am I to assume you know those names and their significance to history?"

Kuka nodded. "Groves and Oppenheimer were the key figures in the *Manhattan Project.* Are you saying these documents are Albright's history and involvement with FDR and the building of the atomic bomb?"

"That's exactly what we determined. I was instructed by a top-level source to secure Bell and Brooks and get the documents. The plans were set and executed. I arranged for a Spec-Op team to perform the mission and deployed them one evening under the cover of darkness. Everything was fine until Nurse Bell panicked and ran. That's when one of our overzealous operators shot her in the back."

Kuka was shocked. "Seriously? Collateral damage?"

"It gets worse. Brooks reacted instinctively and killed all my operators in seconds. Our intel team forgot to thoroughly research his background, and we walked into this assignment not knowing he was an experienced *Delta Force* member from Bragg who was recuperating from physical and emotional wounds while deployed in Afghanistan."

"What happened to Brooks?"

"Before I could get a cleaning team on site, the police arrived. The crime scene was closed to the public. It was a bloody mess. Everyone was dead. It seems one of my men squeezed off a round during the incident that eventually killed Brooks. The situation was passed on to the military and kept out of the news."

"What about the documents?"

DeLorean frowned. "They were gone. We do not know who cleaned up the mess, but they took the documents. We thought this was the end until Kiki saw the pictures on my desk the other day. Now, I don't know what to think. I haven't reported this to anyone. I wanted to see what you found. Which brings us to breakfast."

Kuka gazed at him. "I will keep trying, but I think this case has gone cold. By the way, there is one question I have that hasn't been answered."

"What's that?"

"What will be done with Albright if we find him?"

"Albright holds all the keys to all the issues. Including all the people involved. He must be kept alive."

"So, my mission isn't just about Albright? It includes people who interacted with him. Why are they important?"

"That's not for you to know."

Kuka saw the change in her brother's demeanor. His expression projected the seriousness of the operation. "Ok. I will continue my quest even if it goes cold."

DeLorean nodded. "Thank you. We must remain diligent. Let's get out of here. My butt hurts after sitting too long in this wooden chair. By the way, thanks for buying breakfast. You are a wonderful sister."

Kuka laughed. "Wow! I got top-secret story time, an ugly scowl, and I must buy breakfast. What a privilege."

"Let me remind you. This conversation never happened!" She nodded. They exited and headed to their respective offices.

RENEWED FOCUS - Chapter 12

Bobby began the day by calling for an impromptu meeting with the team. The activities in Germany concerned him, and he wanted the team to focus on the communications to see if anything spilled over the border into America. The increasing attacks from radical organizations motivated by anarchy and the overtaking of governments were contagious and could not be ignored. This was becoming a routine that led to wars. After some relaxed chatter, Bobby called the meeting to order. He began outlining the details of the German operation and the discovery of how deep the participants ranged from the simple to the elite. This was a warning for law enforcement and counterterrorism units. Members with unlimited financial resources, combined with unlimited financial and social influence, would make it difficult to stop growth; more money always meant more problems. After asking if anyone had questions, Gold chimed in. "What about other nations? Should we restrict our radar to Germany or broaden our perspective?"

Bobby nodded. "That's a significant question and consideration. I wanted to avoid stretching our resources too thin. I'm open to suggestions. I have total confidence in this team, so please share anything you think might help."

Martinez began. "Sir, we can handle it. I suggest we divide Europe into sectors and assign each sector to a team member. This would allow us to individually focus on a specific area without overlapping and wasting resources while collectively reviewing our discoveries."

"That's possible. I like it. How about the rest of the team? Do we start with this?"

Everyone nodded in agreement. "Ok. I'll compose a division of the areas into sectors, then call for a meeting to distribute the assignments before the end of the day. This assignment will require us to meet every morning to review information and details. We cannot assume or take anything for granted. We will search and assess each other's information for related and/or overlapping connections that may reveal threats or open the door to additional issues. Questions or considerations?"

After a quick scan of their faces, Bobby responded. "Outstanding. Before we go, I want to say how impressed I am with each of you as we continue to combat cybercrime and complete our transition as another facet of the *United States Cyber Command* (USCYBERCOM). Let's get back to our duties until I make the assignments. I will announce it when we meet this afternoon. I'm glad to be back! Dismissed."

William Martin was enjoying the walk under the clear blue sky. In his quest to find answers, he ignored his hunger pangs, but his stomach audibly broke the serenity to remind him of why he was walking. He laughed to himself as he realized the last photo he examined provided a clue to his search. It revealed the same clue all the other photos provided…nothing! He felt like a dog chasing its tail. Moving quickly, but getting nowhere. The week had been a waste of time. He needed to dismiss the negativity and realign his plans, purpose, and goals. As he arrived, a server greeted him and offered a table. He sat at the same table as the first time, thanks to Sheppard. He ordered a bottle of water and the fish with chips platter. His stomach reminded him again of his purpose. He patted it with his right hand and smiled, thinking in a few minutes, you will be thrilled. The server returned and placed the bottle and platter before him. "Enjoy the meal. I will return in a few minutes to check on you." William nodded. "Thank you." And took his first bite. He reflected on how and what brought him back to this location. A meeting with a man named Sheppard who could have killed me but introduced me to a wonderful dish just minutes away from my office. He let the flavor tantalize his taste buds before swallowing. He spoke aloud to himself. "That is delicious." Then he heard a voice behind him. "Yes, it's very delicious, and please don't turn around." He immediately recognized the voice and did exactly as told…he didn't turn around. "To what do I owe the honor, Mr. Sheppard?"

"I thought today would be the perfect time for us to get together at our favorite eating establishment."

William nodded. "I don't know about perfect, but this is a wonderful place to get fish with chips while unexpectedly meeting interesting people. Thank you for your generosity and the introduction to this platter."

"My pleasure. I normally don't pay for lunch on the first date, but I made an exception for you. By the way, that's the only meal you will get from me."

William laughed. "It's comforting to know you have a sense of humor and broke dating protocol for me."

"Consider yourself special. By the way, speaking of special, have you found it yet?"

The question caught William off guard. "Have I found what yet?"

"The answer?"

William was intrigued. "The answer to what?"

"The documents you have examined revealed nothing and the photos you examined revealed nothing. Therefore, your time and research have revealed nothing. Everything you have done has provided nothing. As you walked here, I'm sure you realized this and questioned if you would ever find something."

William was immediately out of his comfort zone. Normally he was the expert who asked questions, interrogated people, and knew everything about them and the situation. However, at this moment, he felt transparent and vulnerable. He was experiencing negative emotions, but knew Sheppard had established who was in charge of the conversation. William was confident Sheppard was not here to take his life, and resigned himself to the fact he had no choice but to comply and see where this was going. "I don't know what you are talking about."

"How's the fish?" William's thoughts were broken and directed at the fish. He realized Sheppard was not a typical operator. His diversion to temporarily sideline the topic was used to reinforce who directed the conversation. He was impressed. "The fish is delicious. Thank you for asking."

"Continue to eat. I want to make this a dinner theater mystery moment that will help you fill in some gaps. I'm sure you will appreciate the show. Unfortunately, the cast of characters cannot be revealed to you."

William was beside himself as the master technician created an engaging mental picture that drew him in while evasively using metaphors in a cloak-and-dagger cover. "Thank you. I'm sure I will enjoy the meal and the presentation." He took another bite as Sheppard began.

"Did you find out why Churchill summoned Albright?"

William almost choked on the food. How could Sheppard know this? He never shared his investigation with anyone. He shook his head. "No."

"I didn't think so because there is no evidence of their meeting or even why. However, to answer your questions, they met."

William spoke around the food in his mouth, "How would you know that? How do you know I am seeking answers to this if I have never disclosed this to anyone?"

"Relax. I'm sure you, as an expert in espionage, know the game. Stay one step ahead, always be in control, never give up your sources, and always have the upper hand. Stop asking questions and trying to figure out who I am. Eat your food and embrace what I am going to share with you. Appreciate the fact you are here enjoying another delicious platter and not sitting in the basement looking through hundreds of documents for answers that don't exist! I'm saving you time and discouragement. By the way, you are welcome!"

William could not ignore the fact that Sheppard was correct. He was puzzled that even while addressing top-secret issues, Sheppard made jokes. "Thank you. I appreciate the platter that I am paying for and your knowledge of what I need."

He could hear Sheppard smirk. "Now you are in the right mental state to remember the details of what I came to share."

William nodded. "It's comforting to have someone say you've wasted a week of your life running around in the dark looking for a light switch while blindfolded."

"I like that! Running around in the dark while blindfolded, looking for a light switch. Do you mind if I use that in the future?"

Sheppard shook his head. "Not at all!"

"Great! With this, let me turn on the light and remove the blindfold for you. I know you are looking for the purpose, the reason, Churchill summoned Albright. As previously stated, there is no evidence of their meeting, date, time, or location; however, they met."

William continued to eat as Sheppard held his utmost attention.

"Your job is to review field reports and determine if there are threats or circumstances that can become political issues. To read between the lines, you are a professional intelligence officer with vast knowledge of counter operations and engagements. We share a common vocation. We are expected to fill in the blanks, produce evidence of threats, and find solutions to quickly extinguish them. I've looked into their eyes too!"

William knew completely that Sheppard was more than he initially imagined. Sheppard was no ordinary, run-of-the-mill operative if there ever was such a person. Behind him was a man who shared the exemplary skills of investigations, interrogation, combat, and field experiences while casting light on his dead-end search for clues and adding some humor. His statement of looking into their eyes was used by everyone who had a face-to-face encounter killing someone; you never forget the look in their eyes as their life ends. It's a forever reminder of what eventually awaits you when your number comes up. This was the irony of espionage. It was at this moment William realized he was speaking to the best operator he had ever met, and he had met many operators in his lifetime.

"Albright was summoned by Churchill to address a growing concern that was discovered after the war and made every nation in the world reluctant to trust the United States. Truman had the bomb, used it on other humans, rubbed it in Stalin's face, and could use it on anyone who did not comply with the desires and demands of the United States. This situation became the foundation of the *Cold War*. FDR encouraged the creation of the most destructive weapon known to man as a tool for peace, but as sole owner, the United States had a tremendous advantage in controlling the world. Many leaders feared this unique power could cause the President to become a bully who could vaporize anyone who challenged them or questioned their motives." William was processing Sheppard's words and was in awe of the information. Who was Sheppard, and how did he have this information, especially since there were no documents or evidence of the meeting? Was he an American? Possibly, but the genius of Sheppard would never allow his nationality to be revealed. Was Sheppard a nationalist operative devoted by his allegiance to one country or a double agent? It was obvious he was a consummate professional who had vast experience dealing with people. William knew he was the understudy, yet he tried to read Sheppard's words, understand, and interpret his interaction as he interrogated every word Sheppard spoke. Then he was blindsided.

"I know you are looking for any clue of who I am. Who I work for, and what my purpose is with you. You don't trust me, but you have professional respect for me because of our common positions, experiences, and engagements. You also appreciate my information. After all, if you had continued down this rabbit hole into oblivion, your self-confidence would have suffered because you failed, and failure is something you detest. So, stop the analysis of trying to figure out who I am. Your piece-by-piece evaluation of my words will not help you. It will be a waste of time, just like your quest to find evidence of Albright and

Churchill's meeting. The only information you will get today will be specific to the meeting. Please continue to listen carefully."

William could not fathom the conversation and how Sheppard knew exactly what to say and when to say it. He was a master of psychological warfare; perhaps he was a member of a Psy-Ops team. "You know me well. Please continue."

Sheppard was confident. "As I was saying, the unique power held in the hands of Truman created fear amongst other leaders. Stalin knew the only solution to the bomb was to make a bomb. Oppenheimer had released the mechanics of the bomb to the Soviets as a gesture to ensure no single nation had the power to control the world, which, although politically chivalrous, he destroyed his credibility and ostracized himself from any further nuclear endeavors."

> *The divide between the Soviets and Americans quickly expanded into a chasm.*

"In fear of losing the advantage, America embraced Nazi war criminals and sought their experience in rocket technology, biological weapons, medical experimentation, and psychological warfare. *Operation Paperclip* was the secret underground railroad to bring war criminals into America as expert contributors to the military-industrial complex. The United States wasted no time in locating every valuable German asset, especially doctors and scientists. Unfortunately, the officers who failed to have these skills were put before the public and executed as a reminder of what happens to non-essential people who engage in war crimes. Ironic isn't it? The United States created a dog and pony show of hypocrisy as they executed the useless Nazis and kept the useful Nazis; even though both had taken part in war crimes. It was unknown to the Americans, but the same people who murdered and experimented on millions were fast-tracked citizens. It seemed the passion to gain biological weapons and medical technology was more important than restitution for the families who lost loved ones to the heinous acts performed by these evil men and women. The blind eye of necessity took precedence over morality. The tools of war designed to kill become the assets to help humanity…war is ironic and shows how we put our best foot forward and use it to kick people when they are down." William sensed Sheppard had moved.

"That's all I have to say for now. It was nice to see you. I hope this information enlightened you. Remember, I'm not buying today. Do not turn around. Do not try to find out who I am. You will hear from me. Have a good day." William continued to eat without looking around. He did not want to compromise their meeting because the information Sheppard provided was invaluable. He was overwhelmed with the information Sheppard shared. William dabbed this mouth with the napkin. The meal was delicious and the unexpected company, although initially disturbing, provided immeasurable assistance that helped him answer the question of the meeting and encourage his investigation. Sheppard had helped him in two areas: fish with chips and verified Albright had met with Churchill. The question of why remained.

INNOCENCE LOST - Chapter 13

As promised, Bobby called the team together at 1600 and distributed each assignment and related sector. Everyone was onboard and have their first collective meeting, which would occur each day at 0900, in two days. This was the beginning of a new perspective on critical thinking, observation, and spying. After the meeting, Bobby returned to his office, finished packing Chang's personal effects, and called it a day. After arriving at the motel and showering, he was ready to relax before meeting Marty later for a review of her notes. He needed some alone time, so he placed his *Bose 700 Noise Canceling* headphones over his ears and lay on the bed. The music of *Tangerine Dream* filled his mind with synthesized music that connected perfectly with his subconscious. He fell asleep.

After Dr. Martinez had secured the vault, Marty said goodbye and turned to leave for the day. Dr. Martinez interrupted her. "Marty. Do you have a minute?"

"Of course. How can I be of assistance?"

"Dad, I mean Dr. Albright wants us to meet for breakfast here at 0700 tomorrow. He will provide the food and beverages. How does that sound?"

"That is a wonderful surprise. Of course, I'm fine with that. Thank you for asking. Is anyone joining us?"

"My son and Bobby."

Marty smiled. "That's great! Thank you for the invitation. I mean, please thank Dr. Albright for the invitation."

"Of course. Dad feels like you and Bobby are family. He is very reserved about venturing out of his comfort zone, so that says volumes about you both."

"I am honored to be considered so highly. Wow! I look forward to having a family breakfast. Thank you. I'll see you in the morning." Today was slightly different for Marty. Instead of securing all the documents, she had taken a few pages with her notes to review with Bobby later in the evening. There was something about Albright's documents and his details that intrigued her. She couldn't pinpoint it, but something was different, and she wanted Bobby's perspective.

An hour later, the tone was subtle and intensified until Bobby's eyes opened. He knew the music would be hypnotic and put him to sleep. Setting the alarm was necessary because Marty would kick his butt if he missed this meeting. She felt there was something she discovered in Albright's notes, possibly hidden or cryptic, that she needed to share. He understood her passion for addressing issues and quietly appreciated them; her passion brought them into this situation.

Bobby gathered himself, splashed his face, brushed his teeth, and headed to the meeting with Marty. After knocking on the door, Marty greeted him with her signature smile. He walked in and sat on the couch, noticing the plate with two sandwiches and BBQ chips. "Thank you for the food."

Marty looked at him. "Those are for me!"

The smile left Bobby's face. "Oh! Forgive me for assuming you cared."

Marty laughed. "They are for you, crazy man! You are most welcome. Enjoy them. I had a feeling you would be hungry since we practically live together."

Bobby realized she was correct; there wasn't much they did not know about each other. With all their interaction and duties, he failed to realize they had grown to know and appreciate each other's skills and friendship. "I appreciate everything you do for me. Thank you."

Marty valued Bobby's sincerity and gratitude. "Thank you. I guess we never realized the insight and closeness we have developed."

Bobby nodded. "I agree. So, what is the urgency of this meeting? What do you need to share with me?"

"Eat your food first. I want your utmost attention and don't want to hear you talking and eating."

Bobby laughed. "I guess we know each other very well." They laughed.

As Bobby ate, Marty left and returned with a small stack of papers topped with a legal pad and pen. She placed them on the coffee table, separated them, and sat as Bobby finished his meal.

Bobby wiped his mouth with a napkin. "Ok. Let's get started." As he sat up and placed his elbows on his knees.

Marty smiled and picked up the legal pad. "Let me begin with this. As I was reviewing Albright's post-World War II peace accord documents and concerns, I noted the division between America and the Soviet Union surfaced. Albright has always been meticulous and detailed with everything. He has a mental template that accurately elaborates on every event. Today, however, I saw something different in his notations. His composition template changed as his normally predictable robotic details took on a personal air of concern, which was outside of anything he has composed. It seemed something within the *Potsdam Agreement* influenced changes to Albright's systematic details; subtle variations also seemed to appear in his notations after attending the *Yalta Conference*. This deviation addressed certain concerns he believed could lead to more conflicts, even wars, between countries now that other nations had the bomb."

Bobby wiped his hands with the napkin. "Please share the pages where you saw the change in his authoring. I'm curious to see what affected his perception of diplomacy." Marty handed him the pages and he read.

As Bobby read, Marty spoke. "The first prominent concern Albright recognized was disinformation and misinformation regarding truth between the Soviets and Americans. Skewing the truth was becoming the foundational tool to motivate the masses using fear. The first issue of fear is the atomic bomb and world dominance by the one owner. That '*King of the Hill*' mindset shown by Truman influenced and sculpted the psyche of every person in the world, not just leaders, to realize America was a one-nation superpower. Albright noted the world would never be the same as we entered the era of self-annihilation and misinformation. The motivation to preserve a country against nuclear attack had begun; money and resources were available. Albright added how newspapers began the transition from local gossip to bringing information or misinformation (yellow journalism) to the people. These small news sources began the paradigm shift to skew facts and influence fear. Unfortunately, this prompt change confused readers by what they read, and that's when the editors became the composers of articles that shaped stories into a tool of mind control. When I read what was happening, I was shocked. I wondered who was behind this twisted truth philosophy of controlling the masses. Albright didn't exactly reveal that, but he subtly noted the connection."

Bobby nodded. "Let me read this perspective from Albright to you. He said, 'I know it might sound crazy but if you look closely and listen to my words, you're going to see exactly what has happened over the past 100 years and realize that people embrace sources of misinformation as long as it brings psychological comfort; it's part of our psyche, the search for inner peace, to have faith and trust that everything will be fine. It's part of who we are and creates a dangerous vulnerability to be controlled.'"

Marty exclaimed. "I understand! Yes, as the news goes, so do the people!"

Bobby nodded, "Exactly! Create the mindset that everything is fine, and people venture out and have fun. Create the mindset of fear and they stay home and disconnect from society. Does this sound familiar?"

Marty rolled her eyes. "It's like watching the five o'clock news every day."

Bobby half-grinned.

Marty continued. "Even though Albright composed these notes decades ago, he had the insight and perspectives of how any form of social media allows the agenda of a few to control the masses. Which makes the ignorant the victims of emotional control. Unfortunately, this falls directly into the lap of young and impressionable people who cannot see it. They respond emotionally and their actions and mindsets are correlated with the information they receive. Negative information equates to negative reactions; conversely, positive information equates to positive reactions. Even with a world of information at our fingertips, most of these impressionable people cannot invest the time and effort to research the truth. Big Brother has discovered their weaknesses and capitalizes on them every day through social media, news, teachers, and parents. These kids don't have time to be kids! Technology has disconnected them from reality. The lies are fed through their eyes, their ears, and their emotions, especially using resources that present information in a more palatable form of mass media indoctrination 24/7/365. Besides news agencies, advertisers and marketers have also jumped on the bandwagon of producing visual stimuli that taps into their psyche of wants and needs to new levels outside of Maslow's hierarchy. Self-image and self-esteem are their *Achilles Heels* which open their minds to the lies and facades designed to get them into compliance, to compete, then purchase more products to fill their selfish desires to become social superstars and influencers. Misdirection is a resource, a psychological tool, used to control people as they remain in a constant mental state of emotional dependence on social media and status. This dependency causes depression and negativity for those unable to attain the perfect social image, body, popularity, mentality, and attire. These marketing schemes encourage failure, leading to the distribution of medication and huge profits for big pharma and investors. This was Albright's second turning point."

Bobby looked up. "Albright was on target with what we are experiencing today regarding the use of fear shared via news platforms, technology, and psychology to skew information and direct the people like sheep. Looks like the Doc has a clairvoyant side to him for recognizing direction based on misdirection. I agree with you. His normal recording of events seems to have taken a subtle turn, as evidenced by his outlining these two high-profile meetings with the big three and their incorporation of fear of getting whatever they want. Now, back to our purpose."

Stalin already knew the details and turned a cold shoulder towards Truman.

"Albright recorded. 'I can't fathom why Truman would taunt Stalin.' Maybe there was more to their relationship than we know. Regardless, it pushed the Russians away and their cold shoulder became the start of the *Cold War* that influenced the greatest paradigm shift in history as every nation sought the bomb. Cultures, considerations, and concerns immediately changed after the *Potsdam Agreement*. It's interesting how an event scheduled to promote peace and help rebuild countries destroyed by war began another war perspective never imagined before. The photographs showed the big three seated next to each other, stoic and silent. Their stature endorsed Albright's concern that post-WWII allies would go their separate ways after the bomb. He was correct. Fear is the best motivator to increase military might. Heck, we established and embraced that mentality during WWII. Americans showed solidarity in the face of fear, which motivated them to collectively gather tires, food, metals, nylons, and anything that could produce materials of war; all necessary to protect men and women fighting on two battle fronts and those at home."

Fear became the motivational catalyst!

Marty stood and paced in the room. "Keep reading, please. I want to hear what else you see and think."

Bobby was focused as he continued to read. Ten minutes later, he looked up and handed the papers to Marty, who placed them on the kitchen table. "This is something we recognize decades later, but it was perceived as an insurmountable endeavor that has only grown larger. Albright emphasized this and added the perspective fear was the beginning of the end regarding our former comfort and peace of mind; the world had changed and so did the perception of survival. Every day newspapers heralded changes in the economy, the military, and the newest mental distraction...the *Cold War*. The Soviets led the race to use fear with *Pravda* (translated truth)...their nationalist newspaper, which was far from anything true. Inner peace was a thing of the past as fear of war, the bomb, capitalism, and communism took center stage. The factors became the norm that fueled higher taxes and larger budgets to create bigger armed forces, bigger bombs, bigger fallout shelters, and bigger bank accounts. The adage, '*To the victor the spoils*' became the new philosophy in Washington, DC, even during peacetime, if there was peacetime. Albright targeted the center stage and peripheral issues that lead to the formation of the military-industrial complex. War replaced agriculture as America's greatest contributor to the national economy as arms sales to allies grew. The war machine became huge as the military-industrial complex continued to grow. Inevitably, wars would become commonplace as combat resources and supplies flooded the world while a select group of people become rich, the politicians and weapons manufacturers. Anyone with a passion and the ability to motivate people became a threat to world peace. It seemed the model created by Hitler and the *Third Reich* was embraced by more followers than expected, which included the leaders of the United States."

The three transformative leaders represented power, politics, and prowess.

"With the bomb, countries could be bullied to surrender their oil, gold, food, and safety out of fear. The ability to divide, conquer, or embrace an alliance with smaller countries became easy and contributed to the dynasty of those with the most resources and weapons. Division and dissension were spurred on the foundation of fear, power, and protection. These words became the mantra that continues to motivate people throughout the world to open their wallets and throw away their money, hoping their government, or any government, would protect them from all evil enemies. This mentality played perfectly during the *Cold War,* as the United States and the Soviets shared the mentality to coddle smaller counties into their safe havens of deceit, which produced a psychological dependency on the host nation. As the power expanded from atomic weapons, the diversity of chemical and biological weapons added to the ability to wipe out entire civilizations in minutes. It didn't matter where you lived. All that mattered was how each government used mind control, using the most elementary source in humanity…fear!"

Marty sat. She added her perspective on how *Operation Paperclip* prompted efforts of Germans to escape the Soviets, by seeking help from the United States by helping the United States, noting how critical it was to get ownership of the German geniuses before the Soviets. Marty sat back and painted the perspective of how a war would pit man against man as enemies one day, and the next they could lay their weapons down and become allies. Ironically and expected, the Soviets cut ties with America as German nationals were embraced by America. Life was a paradox of confusion within itself. In return, America would get the most intelligent scientists in the world from Germany, while the Russians sought assistance from Jewish scientists and a rumored blueprint from J. R. O.

Bobby stood. "The breadth and depth of these events changed life forever. People would never be the same nor see things as they once were. We became the children of nuclear threats."

Marty nodded. "Now, decades later, these issues are still front and center."

"I agree!"

They sat in silence for a few minutes before Marty blurted out, "We have breakfast tomorrow. I almost forgot to tell you."

"Breakfast? Where and with who?"

"Dr. Albright is treating us with breakfast at 0700 tomorrow at the Smithsonian. Dr. Martinez and her son will attend, too. Dr. Albright sees us like family members now."

"Really? That is amazing. He seems like a man who has a very limited inner circle."

"That's what Dr. Martinez suggested too! I am honored to be considered so highly."

"I'm still digesting this. I don't know what to say, except I hope he has eggs and bacon."

Marty laughed. "You are crazy. How about we watch some television?"

"Sounds great to me. We need a break from all the historical and contemporary drama."

Bobby left two hours later and, before hitting the rack, texted the team that he and Martinez would be predisposed until 0900. The pillow felt so inviting.

BREAKFAST - Chapter 14

After battling traffic and suffering from hanger, Bobby entered the hall and immediately took in the wonderful aroma of breakfast. He accepted the offer as a very kind gesture from Albright; a positive influence because his mouth was watering. He walked into the kitchenette and was greeted by the early birds with smiles on their faces. "Good morning Dr. Martinez, Sergeant Martinez, Marty, and, of course, our short-order cook, Dr. Albright," who turned and smiled. Everyone except the chef was seated in front of empty plates exchanging glances as Bobby sat and looked at the countertop, surprised to see pancakes, bacon, sausage, and toast all carefully arranged on platters. Albright began placing the platters on the table and took egg orders that ranged from scrambled to over easy. After a few minutes, everyone had their food, including the eggs, on their plates. Albright dispensed with his apron and joined the group. Bobby bowed his head and silently prayed as Albright and Sergeant Martinez joined him. Marty knew the routine as she and Dr. Martinez patiently waited.

Albright lifted his head. "Let's enjoy our time together. Thank you for joining me."
Almost as if orchestrated, everyone thanked him. Bobby loved his eggs over easy and immediately grabbed some hot buttered toast and dipped it into the runny egg yolk. He was surprised that everything was cooked perfectly and looked at Albright. "This is incredible! We have discovered another of your many talents."

Albright smiled. "Thank you, but cooking is a hidden passion few people are aware I enjoy. The kitchen gives me a respite from the tension and drama of my position. I'm surprised I don't weigh 500 pounds." Everyone laughed.

Marty raised her glass of orange juice. "Let's have a toast to the chef and recognize his talents." The glasses of orange juice came together with a slight ring as they said, "Cheers!" Bobby looked around and realized he was out of his normal element. He couldn't remember the last time he shared a group meal with non-military members. This was a wonderful time that he had never expected. He felt the emotions of happiness fill him as he raised a piece of toast. "How about another toast to the cook?" Laughter filled the room.

Albright nodded in agreement. "Bobby, you do not know what you just proposed. You took one of the most significant items in American culture and are unaware of its contributions."

Bobby was puzzled. "Ok, where are you taking us with this puzzle?"

Albright's smile broadened. "I love trivia, and this is one of the most significant moments in our culture and psyche."

Bobby raised the piece of toast. "Are you saying toast is a significant contribution to the American culture and psyche?"

Albright nodded. "Not a significant contribution, one of the most important. By the way, it's not the toast, it's the bread."

Marty raised her toast and gently waved it. "Isn't bread a staple in every culture? Why would you make a distinction about our bread?"

Albright nodded. "Great question Marty. Yes, bread is used in various forms around the world. I would like to take a moment to share some interesting things about bread in America, so please allow me to share this. Upstairs is a wonderful invention that changed the face of eating bread and American culture."

Everyone exchanged glances. Bobby smiled. "Here, in the Smithsonian?"

Albright smiled. "Yes. An invention few appreciate, but created a distinct mindset that influenced Americans to remain resolute during World War II."

Sergeant Martinez spoke. "The toaster?"

Albright laughed. "Not in this specific case, but that was another important contribution. As I noted, there is a machine in this facility that changed and motivated people in some of our darkest and most demanding times. What were the things that influenced Americans? The first was sliced bread."

Bobby smiled. "Really? Isn't there an adage, '*It's the greatest invention since sliced bread?*'"

"Yes. That phrase was coined by comedian *Red Skelton* and became part of our common vernacular. As I was saying, this institution is the home of the machine that changed the face of bread in America."

> *Everyone was focused on Albright's presentation. It seemed breakfast had become a lesson in American trivia.*

Albright continued. "In 1917, a jeweler by the name of Otto Rohwedder designed and created a prototype machine to mechanically slice bread. Unfortunately, a fire destroyed his prototype and blueprints. He continued his quest to create the machine. He was met with criticism and skepticism from both bakers and consumers. Fortunately, he never wavered. His dream persevered in the face of negativity, and he created the first automatic commercial bread slicer on July 6, 1928, in Chillicothe, Missouri. It seemed the Iowa-born, Missouri-based businessman made his dream a reality after refining the prototype into a power-driven, multi-bladed bread slicer and putting it into service at the *Chillicothe Baking Company*."

Dr. Martinez spoke. "Dad, that is an incredible story. I knew nothing about Mr. Rohwedder or that his invention was here. I won't even ask how you know about him."

Albright raised a piece of toast. "Hold on! Before we have a toast," Everyone laughed. "There is more to the story of bread. During World War II, Americans sacrificed many essentials to support the troops. FDR proposed that bread would become another sacrifice. However, the unexpected pushback from the people to keep their beloved bread forced him to change the decision. Bread was one of the most cherished and fundamental staples that provided emotional positivity and stability to people during the war. As the attaché to FDR, I witnessed the Cabinet members debate to keep bread on the table. A decision that motivated and endorsed a positive mentality in most Americans. Incredibly, bread and the automatic slicer survived the Great Depression and World War II. So, sliced bread became an unsung hero of World War II. Even though bread has passed the tests of time, it became a rock star when sliced and contributed to the American spirit."

"Dad, that is incredible. I would have never imagined that bread, sliced or not, would have such a dramatic impact on our culture, especially during the war. Thank you for sharing this with us."

Albright nodded and picked up the bread. "Now we will toast the moment." Everyone held their bread high. "Our toast to the toast!" They touched toast and smiled. Albright knew this moment allowed them insight into how the smallest things have the greatest impact on our lives. Something he had grown to appreciate and value.

Everyone agreed it was an unexpected, enlightening, and incredible backstage story of history and the American spirit. After finishing, they pitched in to clean the kitchenette and dispose of the trash. This was the first of hopefully several breakfast gatherings. Afterward, they left for their respective duties. Albright was thrilled.

PART THREE

THE TRUTH PREVAILS

CLEAN UP - Chapter 15

DeLorean sat, deep in thought, reflecting on his breakfast meeting with Kuka. He violated security protocol, which took him outside his scope of authorization to share ultra-top-secret information. He trusted his sister, but knew there would always be the possibility she could be forced to talk if ever captured and tortured. He knew the importance of keeping secrets, especially after the operations of the 6th floor were leaked. The discovery of illegally imprisoning American citizens who were retired covert operators made the President's blood boil. His administration was ridiculed by veterans, along with active and past covert operators. He accepted responsibility and apologized to family members profusely. Regardless of his position, he knew someone low on the food chain would be sacrificed and fed to the political and news lions. He could not afford the negative shadow that veiled his popularity and could keep him from getting a second term in the White House. He garnered every political and military support possible, asking them to parade before the cameras to help exonerate him. DeLorean looked back at the situation that caused all the negativity and drama that threatened his career...Albright's escape! He replayed how news of the 6th-floor atrocities spread like wildfire. Fortunately, it was corralled into a small, tight circle comprising only those involved. Getting everyone removed and reconnecting with their families took precedence.

  The President was incensed that a black-ops mission of this morbid degree was happening under his nose and without his knowledge. He swore heads would roll and the responsible parties would be dealt to the highest degree of severity. The incarcerated and their families were forced to remain silent regarding their captivity and their involvement with any prior operators or news agencies. To ensure the issue remained a secret, every person was compensated beyond expectations. How did this collection of people end up on the 6th floor? DeLorean was the taskmaster who orchestrated the discovery, identification, capture, and incarceration of every person who took residency on the 6th floor.

In the end, some walked out, some rolled out, and some were never heard from again. This was the irony of espionage and permanent retirement.

Anyone who died on the 6th floor was buried under an anonymous name in an undisclosed location. Their families never knew what happened to them; however, just like the survivors, every family received a generous payment from an unknown trust account; ironically it was a trust account amid lies and deception. DeLorean was intrigued by the success of how unexpected money, in large bills, changed morale and made death so much easier to accept for the family.

These thoughts and reflections brought him to this moment, the culmination of his prior and present duties. He remained in the same building, in the same office, and in the same chair. The only thing that wasn't the same was his new command. He was reassigned and given another series of orders. Today he would not be seeking former operators to be taken from freedom and placed into a sterile, spartan room at an undisclosed location in a coma to die. That was his prior assignment. Today he would find everyone from the list and at the right time and place they would die of natural causes, a car accident, a plane crash, falling down a flight of stairs, or other accidents to remove all questions regarding their cause of death. Nothing changed except their manner of death. He would sit in the shadows, orchestrating and scheduling each incident, not waiting for them to eventually die in bed. The trick to eliminating other operators was knowledge of their lifestyle and timing. Each would die doing something they enjoyed or in an accident. Accidents were the best avenue of termination because there were witnesses and witnesses provided facts…another bitter irony of the job. Each would die at different times, in different locations, and under different circumstances; however, the results were the same…everyone would die, and DeLorean would complete the mission he began. He would reestablish his integrity and continue to climb the ladder of promotions while ensuring no one compromised any secret or said anything because dead men tell no tales. The former "Sky Soldier" was now codenamed, "Hunter."

He never revealed his authority or activities to anyone outside of the office. Just like Bobby, he oversaw a small group of specialists who sat in the dark engaged in the dark world of secrecy. The change in his responsibilities added to his skill set, regardless of how morbid, his military portfolio grew with experience in leadership and trust; qualities needed to reach the stars. He removed the first folder from the stack he had organized earlier, nestled in the right corner of his desk. He opened it and looked at the photograph of the former operator. She was a skilled network hacker who helped break into several top-secret Russian, Iranian, and Chinese computer networks. She helped Israel hack into and stop the Iranian nuclear program and release Trojan horse malware that effectively destroyed all data. Unfortunately, she would be involved in an automobile accident in which a large truck would run a stop sign, crashing into the driver's side of her car, and killing her instantly. The stack would never empty, as new files were added to the names and identities of critical operators who would pay the ultimate price for their patriotic services. DeLorean was intrigued about how so many people were expendable after they were no longer needed. He heard rumors regarding the first person to be terminated in this program. Regardless of true or false, conspiracy theories abound in the spy arena regarding a man who went through some of the craziest and deadliest battles of World War II and survived with no wounds or complications, yet died in a freak, post-war car accident while the other two occupants of the vehicle walked away unscathed. General George Patton was a hero. Unfortunately, he had a big mouth and didn't filter his thoughts, which may have made him expendable.

> *Unfortunately, Patton and JFK shared one thing...each mysteriously died.*

DeLorean snapped back to reality and pressed the intercom button. He ordered the new commander of his Spec-Op team to report to his office to receive and review orders for the new mission. After the review DeLorean began the duties of his additional assignment, monitoring changes in the world population. He never questioned the orders of his superiors, but bit his tongue several times in the past to avoid conflict when he felt like challenging the mission.

The only thing regarding this new assignment that intrigued him was the world's population. He was instructed to monitor and compile quarterly numbers on the increase or decrease of population per these predefined areas. He asked if there were additional considerations and the commanding officer told him to consider researching the *Malthusian Theory of Population*. In his years of service, no commander had ever suggested research specific to the operation, which was outside the norm for orders. He took the bait and discovered several interesting considerations regarding the world's population and the *Malthusian Theory of Population*. The first point that took his attention was the premise noted by Thomas Robert Malthus, an English cleric, and scholar, who published his 1798 essay, the *Principle of*

Population, which outlined expected exponential population growth and the ability to maintain sustainable food supplies to feed the people.

Malthus argued there would be a time when the population surpassed the availability of food production, resulting in famine and people dying from food shortages. DeLorean was amazed at how Malthus made such a morbid prediction while the world population was one-quarter of what it is today. He was also impressed by how Malthus had already assigned his name to a situation that could cause a correction of the world's population; the *Malthusian Catastrophe*, which would bring the population level back to a "sustainable number." The irony of the *Principle of Population* was the *Malthusian Trap*. Ironically, people, by nature, help each other and the trap noted that as levels of food production increased to feed the masses, advanced agricultural techniques would be required and created. Unfortunately, there would be the terminal reciprocal of higher populations that would produce food shortages.

Were the considerations of Malthus pure genius of clairvoyance or just a hypothetical consideration of the possible catastrophic loss of life that could result from failing to control the world's population? Regardless of the situation and circumstances, DeLorean knew where this assignment was going. There was a knock on his door. He invited the commander to enter.

CONNECTIONS - Chapter 16

Albright was reviewing the 'Big Picture' as he liked to refer to the tentacles of his operations. No one, not even Dr. Martinez, his daughter, or grandson, knew everything about him. He was an enigma. His mentality and philosophy contributed to him living longer and hopefully dying from natural causes, not from lead poisoning, wandering off into the woods, or a freak car accident. The revelation that Bobby and Marty discovered about Dr. Martinez and her son being family was big, but never to be spoken of. In fact, it was good because it removed any tension about accidentally saying something with a slip of the tongue. Bobby and Marty could be trusted, and the bond between Bobby and Sergeant Martinez was special as Brothers-in-Arms who had fought together.

He spoke with Sheppard earlier regarding his interactions with William Martin. Sheppard told him that Martin seemed more receptive after getting the news that Churchill had met with him, even though there were no documents regarding the meeting. Albright laughed. He knew this information would keep Martin on the hook seeking answers which would open the door for more assistance from Sheppard and get access to the MI6 network. His objectives were going as planned. He thanked Sheppard and told him to stand by until given new orders. Sheppard agreed. Albright sat back and interlocked his fingers behind his head. He smiled.

The Aristocrat was away from his office. He was summoned by one of his high-profile clients to meet in person regarding the task of taking out some trash. These meetings fueled his adrenaline and barbaric bloodlust for removing unwanted people and disposing of them. His curiosity always greeted his anticipation of finding out who the target was, where they were located, and the selected manner of disposal. He relished the opportunity to ensure the job was performed promptly and properly. With each request, his reputation was on the line, and he refused to let anyone do the job. His father always told him, "If you want a job done right, do it yourself." His focus returned to piloting the jet. He loved the enhanced vision system and active side stick controls as he took in the view from Flight Level 500, cruising at 600 knots. Sitting in the left seat of his private *Gulfstream G700* was a dream come true. Regardless of age, no man ever grows up. The only thing that changes is the price of their toys and $75 million seemed to be a bargain price for this jet. This was an added job perk because the clients paid all travel costs. His evil grin returned as he thought, "It's good to be king!"

Martinez and Bobby were the last two people in the office. Everyone else left promptly at 1700. Bobby walked to Martinez's office and asked if he was leaving or had a few minutes to spare. Martinez said he wasn't in a hurry and followed Bobby to his office after he motioned him.

"Have a seat. How's everything going with the sector searches?"

Martinez nodded. "Seems to be going well. Unfortunately, I haven't found anything of value yet."

Bobby sat back and looked Martinez in the eyes. "How good are you at hacking?"

Martinez was surprised by the question. "Hacking? Do you mean network surveillance? Hacking is such a barbaric word."

They laughed. "Sorry! I meant network surveillance. Anyway, I am asking this for a reason."

"I caught that immediately. No one has ever asked me that question. I'm here. What's the plan?"

"Whatever I share with you from this moment forward stays between us. Do you understand?"

Martinez nodded in agreement. "Of course."

"A few months ago, I met with an operator from MI6 at Legoland."

Martinez looked confused. "*Legoland*? Is this a covert cover at a children's store?"

"No. It's the name used by operators in MI6 for headquarters, since the structure looks like it was built with *Legos*. The building design prevents electronic eavesdropping."

"That's interesting how we have evolved from spying to *Legos* to counterespionage using an interlocking toy as a structural model."

Bobby laughed. "That's an interesting perspective. Anyway. Our man inside was promoted from the field to headquarters. I was given the assignment of seeking his professional services from one country to another. I was in full Spanish military attire. After I explained everything to him, he agreed to help. The discovery that Martinez was the grandson of Albright couldn't have been revealed at a better time because Albright arranged the meeting with William Martin. With this, Bobby knew anything about Albright could never be shared, nor let out until this investigation was complete."

> He could not let Martinez know he was spying on his grandfather.

Bobby's questions regarding Chang and Albright consumed his thoughts. There were too many questions, and this was his first step to finding answers. Why did Albright want assistance from Martin? Why would Albright say he knew nothing about the German dragnet and arrests, then make a specific statement about the groups involved? Again, too many questions bounced around in Bobby's head and his passion to find answers was obsessive.

Bobby redirected his attention to Martinez. "So, are you up for a venture of the highest order?"

Martinez smiled. "These are the operations I love. Covert and under the radar. Thank you for bringing me in on the action."

Bobby smiled. "You will not know the gravity of action required from you until you engage in the details of this mission."

Martinez went expressionless. "Is it really that deep?"

"Yes. You say nothing of this to anyone. We cannot afford to lose this small window of opportunity."

"Yes, sir! I will keep this between us."

"You will be told when and where we will meet to talk about this operation. This will be the first and last time we address it in the office. Thank you. Let's go home."

Martinez stood up. "Sounds great to me." As he turned to leave.

"Martinez! Thank you for your dedication. You have always been there for me and are a valued friend, even though the military says we cannot be friends because of fraternization. Our brotherhood is off the grid but in our souls."

"Yes, sir! I understand! Off the record and the grid, sir."

Bobby smiled, "Of course. Off the record and the grid. αδέλφια για πάντα!

Martinez asked. "What's that?"

"Brothers forever in Greek! See you tomorrow, brother."

"I didn't know you spoke Greek."

"Only the important stuff!"

"Always full of surprises. Have a wonderful evening. See you in the morning."

"Of course we will! Thank you!"

HIDDEN TREASURES - Chapter 17

Marty arrived a few minutes early and saw Dr. Martinez in the parking lot. They walked to the office together, chit-chatting about the weather and traffic.

Marty inquired. "How was the Caiaphas event?"

Dr. Martinez's eyes lit up. "It was fantastic! We had renowned archeologists from all over the world join us. The discussions and presentations were incredible. I'm so glad you asked."

Marty smiled. "I'm not that familiar with your field of historical knowledge, but I find it very interesting now that I share my space with you. Do you have any new events scheduled?"

"It's interesting that you should ask. We are expecting some archeological treasures discovered by a team of German and Kurdish archaeologists who uncovered a 3400-year-old *Mittani Empire-era* city on the Tigris River. Since the water levels are currently the lowest ever recorded for the Tigris, this was an unprecedented discovery; an unknown settlement emerged from the waters of the Mosul reservoir early this year. The discovery included a city with a palace and several large buildings that are common *Zakhiku* known to be from the *Mittani Empire* sometime around 1550-1350 BC."

Marty was in awe. "That's incredible how you know the details of the discovery, the artifacts, and the period of history. Holy cow! I feel like I just attended a class in ancient civilizations."

Dr. Martinez smiled. "Get used to it. The artifacts we receive weekly always bring a historical story with them. I never grow tired of working here."

Marty nodded. "That is obvious. When are these artifacts scheduled to arrive?"

"Later today. I can't wait to hold history in my hands. I often associate my passion with those of Indiana Jones."

Marty could see the excitement on Dr. Martinez's face. "That's great. I'm sure you are happy the reservoir water levels dropped."

Dr. Martinez's expression changed. "Not really. This event has never happened in recorded history. Well, in all actuality, it is recorded but as a contemporary entry. This was predicted to happen and believe it or not, we are staring prophecy in the face."

Marty didn't know if she understood the statement or if Dr. Martinez failed to say it correctly. "I'm sorry. I didn't catch what you were saying. Did you say this was previously recorded as an event that would happen?"

"Yes. There are no records that show the Tigris and Euphrates Rivers as having such low water levels, but it was predicted to happen."

Marty stopped walking. "Predicted? You mean like Nostradamus?"

Dr. Martinez stopped and turned back toward Marty. "Kind of, but in the Bible."

Marty was set back. "The Bible? That book filled with stories about God. It is written there. How is that possible?"

Dr. Martinez grinned. "My job here is to research history and any documents that have records that have been verified as fact. I cannot ignore anything that can be proven as evidence of past and even future events. I have reviewed thousands of documents and artifacts for validity. A majority have been rejected, but the sources that are validated remain here for cross-referencing and support."

Marty shifted on her feet. "But I thought the Bible had been proven to be a bunch of stories that have no credibility."

"Not true. Many documents that address religion within various cultures contain historical facts that cannot be ignored. In fact, the Bible is one of the most accurate historical documents we use. I cannot be biased as a researcher. I must seek the sources and glean the content for truth."

Marty meandered. "You said the low water levels of the Tigris and Euphrates were predicted to happen? How long ago was this prediction made?"

"About two thousand years ago, when Paul penned the book of Revelation. Both rivers were mentioned in the first book of the bible, Genesis about five thousand years ago. However, it wasn't until the last book of the Bible, Revelation, that the water levels of these two rivers were mentioned."

Marty interrupted. "So, the first and last books of the Bible introduce the rivers and their water levels from full to empty?"

"Exactly!"

Marty looked down and then regained eye contact. "Why are the water levels in the Book of Revelation so important?"

Dr. Martinez took a big breath. "Their water levels are an indicator of the last days. It is an event that must happen to allow the forces from the east, Gog and Magog, to invade Israel. I'm not saying the Bible is correct, but in all my years as a researcher, this book has provided facts that cannot be debated."

Marty looked scared. "Who are Gog and Magog?"

"Russia and China."

"Russia and China. They recently formed a never before alliance. Are you saying we are in the last days of the world? Is that what Dr. Albright meant about the end times?"

"Dad and I share several common philosophical tenets. He is intelligent with the Bible and believes the content is infallible. I, on the other hand, believe in things that have been proven. So far, the Bible has been correct. I, however, need more facts about prophecy before I'm completely onboard."

Marty placed her hand on the digital reader, and the doors opened. They continued to walk. "That is incredible. I expected nothing like what you just told me. I thought the Bible was a book of fables. You were correct when you said every day we learn something new here. Thank you for sharing this with me. I'm in awe and really don't know how to mentally and emotionally digest everything."

Dr. Martinez smiled. "My pleasure. This is a deep subject. If the words in Revelation are true, things are going to get very interesting as they unfold."

Marty was expressionless. "If they are true, does that mean we are doomed?"

Dr. Martinez was stoic. "If true, we are in for a change in life as we know it."

The color drained from Marty's face. She was speechless.

Dr. Martinez could see her fearful reaction and changed the subject. "Do you want me to contact you when the *Mittani Empire-era* artifacts arrive?"

Marty took a moment to respond. "Sure. I'm curious. Thank you. Well, we had better get to work."

"Yes. We have a job to do. Thank you for the enlightening conversation. I hope I didn't cause too much intensity."

Marty lied. "Oh, no. This was very interesting. Thank you. Have a great day."

They continued to their respective offices.

Sergeant Martinez arrived at 0700 and began reviewing the information he received regarding his sector. Bobby walked in and gave him the head nod to follow him to his office. The timing was perfect because the other team members would arrive at 0730. Bobby motioned him to sit, then closed the door, and sat. "How is the sector/section project going?"

Martinez nodded. "Good. The only thing hot in my area were more arrests in Germany regarding the QAnon and anti-government German protestors."

"That does not surprise me. Ok. Let's get into our new game of espionage, shall we?"

"Yes, sir, but yesterday you said we would not talk about it here."

"Well, in my haste, I forgot a critical piece of information. So, this will be our last meeting in this area."

Martinez laughed. "Outstanding.

Bobby smiled. "I need you to hack. I mean, use your savvy network skills to get into LTC DeLorean's network. Once you have established residency, stay under the radar, and create a shadow account that forwards everything he does to you. Can you do it?"

Martinez was in awe. "Are you ordering me to violate military law, *Uniform Code of Military Justice* (UCMJ), and knowingly enter a secure network to capture and record top-secret intel?"

Bobby nodded with a smile. "That pretty much sums it up!"

"Wow! I never expected this. That won't be easy, but give me a few days to explore my resources and opportunities. You have more faith in me than I expected, and I never dreamed we would be on a covert mission of this magnitude."

"Remember, someone hacked into our system, and we have a map of their IP Addresses even if they are dynamic. I believe it originated with DeLorean. I know you will get this done."

"Thank you. I'll get on it."

"Let me know if you need anything. I have many contacts that we can call upon to help keep this a Black-Op."

"Black-Op? You never mentioned Black-Op."

Bobby smiled. "I would have eventually told you."

Martinez laughed. "I'm glad you were not like this when we were down range. You have gotten us all killed."

"I've learned a thing or two after taking a round. Let's say I've gotten smarter, too!"

Martinez shook his head. "We all have. I'm glad we are still working together."

"Me too! We are blessed! Let's get this show on the road."

Martinez stood. "Yes, sir! Let me know when you need any updates and where we will meet."

Bobby gave a curt salute. "Absolutely! Thank you."

Martinez did likewise and left the office.

After the surprise meeting with Sheppard, Martin sat at his desk, considering what would be his next move in discovering the reason for the meeting between Churchill and Albright. As impulsive as he was to find answers, he would have to put this thought on the back burner because Sheppard told him future contact would provide more details. He hated waiting.

Kuka sat at her desk in the Finnish Embassy. She was staring into space as the frustration of finding nothing consumed her thoughts. There must be something missing. Something out there, hidden in plain sight. She closed her eyes and stepped back in time. The only potential lead was the photos Kiki saw on the desk and swore that she had spoken with Bobby and Marty. She picked up her phone and called her brother. The next question was if he would answer.

"Hello."

"Brother. I need to meet with you tonight. Do you have any plans?"

"I was going on a date with the President's wife, but you just ruined that excursion."

She needed a laugh, and his response provided it. "I'm sorry about that. I'm sure she will understand and make future arraignments with you when he is out of the country. So, do we have a date?"

DeLorean chuckled. "Of course. What time and what are you bringing for dinner?"

"7:00 p.m. and I'll bring KFC."

"That sounds great! I haven't had KFC for a while. Good call! I'll see you at 7:00.

Bobby was reviewing the assignments given to the team when his cell phone buzzed. He looked at the caller ID, UNKNOWN, and ignored the call. Another call immediately followed from the same caller. Bobby did not want distractions and answered. The caller questioned him. "Sir, is this Colonel Roberto Arrollo?"

Bobby was defensive. "To whom am I speaking?"

The caller was persistent. "Is this Colonel Roberto Arrollo? If it is, I have some important investigation information to share with him."

Bobby was immediately engaged. "I am Colonel Roberto Arrollo. Who are you and what information are you speaking of?"

My name is Special Agent Reginald White, and I am the lead investigator for the FBI regarding the possible espionage case of your predecessor, Major Chang."

Bobby sat up in the chair and pressed the phone against his ear. "Go ahead."

Agent White continued. "The incident was investigated fully, and it was determined that Major Chang was not involved in any form of espionage. His history is clean of any issues regarding integrity."

Bobby was speechless. Chang was innocent. Chang killed himself. Why? "During your investigation, did you determine the identity of the Asian man who met Major Chang regularly?"

"Yes. The man is a Chinese national who moved to the United States with an endorsement from a family member."

Bobby felt his stomach tighten. "Who are the man and the family member?"

Agent White responded stoically. "The man is Chi Sing Cho Chang, the uncle of Major Chang. Chang helped him apply for a visa to come to America with the possibility of establishing residency as a person seeking asylum from Chinese persecution. Major Chang was meeting his uncle once during the week to give Chang money to deposit in his bank account because he feared the Chinese government would take his money. The uncle also shared newspapers with Chang because he did not read English and needed help to locate an apartment. Chang would toss the paper after their meetings because he hired an apartment headhunter, unknown to his uncle, who spoke Chinese and knew the area well. Unfortunately, the uncle is now in the middle of getting immigration status but has no money or access to Chang's bank account. This frustration adds to the uncle's devastation that his nephew is dead. He relied on Chang for everything."

Bobby felt like vomiting. He felt the guilt of Chang's death and his uncle's situation rest directly upon his shoulders. Bobby thought, "Why would Chang kill himself if he was innocent? Why didn't I confront Chang first? What could I have done differently?" His thoughts were interrupted by questions from Agent White. "Sir, are you there?"

Bobby reacted. "Yes. I apologize for my silence. I was attempting to fathom what you just shared with me."

Agent White was empathetic. "I understand. When I reviewed the details of the investigation and the conclusion, I was in awe. I can understand why an investigation was started and could blame no one for considering it. This was a textbook scenario that, unfortunately, ended in the life of an innocent man."

"Agent White, will I be getting a copy of the investigation?"

"No. This investigation was requested by your office, but no documentation can be provided. If you have questions, contact me and I will provide any information that is not considered classified."

"I understand. Thank you for your time."

"My pleasure. Is there anything else I can help you with?"

Bobby shook his head. "No. Have a good day."

"You are too."

The call concluded, and Bobby stood to help stop the nausea from filling his gut. His mind was a blur of questions. How could this have happened? Why? Why? Why? He was overwhelmed. He needed to get out of the office and think. He emailed the team he would be out but return soon.

Marty secured the documents in the vault as Dr. Martinez locked the system and verified the security protocols were intact. As they walked toward their offices, Marty looked at Dr. Martinez. "Do you mind if I ask you a personal question?"

Dr. Martinez smiled. "Go ahead."

"You never mention your son's father? Are you divorced? You don't have to answer this. I was curious because, in all our conversations, nothing has been said about him."

Dr. Martinez smiled. "Not a problem. He is dead."

Marty was shocked and immediately went into damage control. "I'm so sorry. I never meant to bring this up. Please forgive me."

Dr. Martinez raised her hand toward Marty's face as a gesture to stop speaking. "It's ok. It's been several years. The apple never falls far from the tree. For some crazy reason, all the men in my family are consumed with danger, living on the edge. They can't be happy doing the mundane things of life. They gravitate toward the danger of military operations as they thrive on the tightrope of life and death. My husband, Buzz, and son are from the same mold. Buzz was always on the leading edge of the action. No mission was too big or dangerous. He had a heart for patriotism and was doing his best as a Soldier. He loved his job and the men he worked with. Unfortunately, he died in combat."

"I'm sorry."

"I was always intrigued by his intelligence; he was a financial guru who would have fit perfectly on *Wall Street* as an investment broker. I believed he would have made millions, but sitting at a desk was like a prison to him. He longed for the outdoors. The rugged terrain of the mountains and ferreting out the enemy. It seems so strange. I haven't said his name for many years. It's always Buzz. I guess that makes him seem alive. Captain Audie 'Buzz' Hall was the love of my life named after World War II hero *Audie Murphy*. He was never a stranger to anyone, and he was always ready to help feed or clothe people. He was my gift from God. He was a special man to me, my son, and our families. He got the nickname because he would always say, '*To infinity and beyond*' every time he jumped out of an airplane. Ironically, he is now in the great beyond for infinity. My wounds will never heal. My tears will never dry. I supported his decision to go to Spec-Ops and every day I second-guess myself. If I would have pushed back, he might be here today."

"You cannot blame yourself for supporting the man you loved. You knew he would have hated sitting at a desk as life passed by for a man destined for a life of military service and sacrifice. You don't know what he did and the lives he saved. Your support of him made life happen. You did what needed to be done."

She looked away as tears began falling from her cheeks onto the floor. "My son is without a father. I am without a husband. The nation is without a hero. The only consolation I have is he died a hero. He died saving lives. He was assigned to the *Green Berets* gathering front-line intel during a secret operation when their team was compromised by a teenager who stumbled upon them. Instead of killing the kid as protocol dictated, my husband let him go, hoping the boy would see the kind gesture of sparing his life. I'm sure the kid was about the same age as our son. Instead, the kid reported their outpost to the enemy, which resulted in a firefight and losing five operators and my husband. He should have stuck to protocol; his compassion was his weakness. Our son was devastated. He vowed to get even, and that anger drove him to the brink of insanity in his quest to become a *Delta Operator*. That's where he met Major Brooks. The major took him under his wing and refined him into a professional soldier. At first, I wasn't too happy, but I realized his skills to kill and survive would be the tools needed to bring him home. Now, here we are engaged in battles never considered before."

"I hear you. The battlefield changes, but wars continue with every generation. It's a never-ending sacrifice of humans and resources. Nobody wins."

They arrived at her office. She sat, took a tissue, and wiped the tears from her eyes. "This is where I hide my hurt. I sit alone in the bowels of the *Smithsonian* and immerse myself in history. A distraction during the day, but the wounds are always open; sensitive to my recollection and pain." She reached into her desk and placed a small *Buzz Lightyear* toy on the desk. "He gave me this before he shipped out on his last deployment. Looking back, it's an omen he knew something was going to happen." She picked up the toy, closed her eyes, and kissed it. This was her moment to remember her husband's love. She looked at Marty. "We best get out of here. Thank you for allowing me to share my innermost hurt with you. I'm glad you asked about Buzz. It keeps him alive in my heart. Marty wiped a tear away from her eye. She felt the pain and saw the importance of cherishing every minute of life. They stood and walked together to the parking lot in silence.

At exactly 7:00 pm Kuka arrived with the KFC as the odor filled the apartment when she placed the bags on the table. DeLorean was giddy with anticipation. "That smells heavenly. Let's dig into this."

Kuka smiled. "I agree with you. This is perfect. Here we are sitting together and getting ready to share in one of our childhood passions...KFC!"

They helped each other remove the food from the boxes and containers. Then shared the dishes and partook in the food. They said nothing as each took in each delicious bite. Ten minutes later, they dabbed the grease from their faces and smiled as each sat back. DeLorean looked at the glow in his sister's eyes. "It's so nice to see you as a child with me. Reminiscing on a KFC meal as the glimmer of light in your eyes sparkled as we shared in the moment of childhood glee. They sat in silence.

Kuka finally spoke. "What happened to us? What happened to our innocence? It seems like a lifetime ago that we were thrilled to eat chicken, laugh, and play. Now, we are calloused by life and our positions. Sometimes I think about where we are and what we have become. Will we ever be normal? Will we ever have children? Will the things we have seen and done catch up to us one day and even out on the playing field? What happens when our number comes up? Will we disappear like the people we are assigned to dispose of?"

DeLorean was taken back. He had never seen his sister show any emotion or question the things she did in her professional career. "You need to relax. We have a purpose and mission. Our lives and careers are not typical, and they will never be normal. We have a mission that requires the killing of some people to ensure the protection of all people. We have a tough mission! Yes, I often think about what you just shared, but it cannot stop us from succeeding, especially since Albright disappeared."

Kuka stared directly into DeLorean's eyes, as if oblivious to his words. "Nobody walks away from what we do. I believe we are as expendable as the people we removed. I wanted to have a family, but I cannot raise my children in the shadow of death. Who knows, maybe one day someone will show up and kill the kids in front of me, then put a 9mm between my eyes. I cannot bear to think of losing my loved ones, yet every day you and I steal the lives of people from their families. Why? Because they dedicated their lives to protecting the United States and when they are no longer needed, we put them down like an old dog. We suck!"

DeLorean sat stoically. "How many times have you thought about this?"

"Too many! My life has been consumed with my passion for promotion and recognition. Now, I'm realizing that once I'm gone, none of what I did will matter. The letters, the promotions, and the bonuses mean nothing. The accolades from my supervisors filled my ears with pride, but no one else shared these moments because they were classified. We don't exist outside of the box we have been put into."

DeLorean recognized the stress Kuka was feeling. She hadn't completed this job; she fell short, and that is never acceptable in this area of work. "Sister!"

She was surprised by her childhood name, which snapped her into reality. "Yes, brother."

We need to relax. A few minutes ago, we were living in a childhood moment of laughter and joy. Let's not forget those happy times. Hang on to the joyous memories of innocence. We must live those moments in fullness. They can never be overshadowed or jaded by our jobs. He stood and walked to Kuka. He took her hands in his and guided her into his arms. They held each other in silence. It has been years since they took the time to hold each other in a gesture of sibling love and support. She cried. The frustration was too much to hold in. DeLorean grabbed some napkins from the table and handed them to her. For 10 minutes she wept as her brother held her. This was their time and moment to help each other. To put the woes of life behind them temporarily and fulfill their purpose as a family. When she stopped crying, she was exhausted, too weak to stand. He escorted her to the couch, where she collapsed onto the cushions. A few minutes later, she was sleeping. He sat looking at his sleeping sister. She stepped outside of her normally iron-clad shell. She was vulnerable tonight and needed a brother, not a professional. He was here for her. In fact, he realized they were both in need of each other. He drifted off into a much-needed time of sleep, too. Tomorrow will be another day. Tonight, was theirs for the taking.

SURPRISE - Chapter 18

Bobby did not return to the office. The information from Special Agent White was replaying in his mind like a broken record. He was overwhelmed by the results. He was overwhelmed that Chang was dead. He was overwhelmed, trying to find answers. Unfortunately, nothing came to mind. He drove until he almost ran out of gas. After filling the tank, he bought a drink and candy bar to fight off the hunger pangs and continued to drive in deep thought. Regardless, he was outside of himself and dealing with guilt. He eventually returned to the hotel, hoping that the excursion would have mentally exhausted him and allowed sleep to take over. He had muted the cell phone ringer and was unaware that Marty had called and texted him several times.

He was not in the right mental state to speak with her.

He texted her a message saying his phone was acting crazy and they would meet tomorrow after work. She asked if he was ok. He texted everything was fine except for a cantankerous cell phone. They slept. Morning came too soon. He awoke, but was immediately greeted by the same emotions he was having before. He was a professional soldier. There were men who were close to him and had lost their lives in combat. He had seen life and death intimately and he questioned why Chang's incident was different. He pondered if his zeal to catch a spy clouded his judgment, which led to a premature investigation of Chang, which contributed to his death. He needed to get control of his emotions and regain focus on the events, and the evidence, to see if there was anything he missed. The renewed focus would put his emotions on the back burner and give him a new purpose. He was ready for the day.

DeLorean arrived at 0800 and sat at his desk. Before he could completely turn toward the computer, he was interrupted. "Sir, we have a data breach!"

He twisted back and looked directly at the NCO standing in the doorway. "What do you mean, a data breach? A hack? How is that even possible?"

The NCO continued. "As we reviewed the network activity last night, it was discovered someone broke into the system one week ago and specifically targeted the server holding the data of all patients and medical staff from the 6th floor."

DeLorean was surprised, which was out of character. "Were you able to determine what they were looking for?"

The NCO nodded. "Yes. They seemed to have reviewed records for staff members Bell, Little Blood, Jenkins, and Brooks. They only read one patient file."

DeLorean interrupted. "Let me guess...Albright?"

"Yes, sir. I won't ask how you know that. However, I need to remind you that all other data storage locations had patients identified by room numbers to maintain identification integrity; no code and no name except on our computers...only. With this, we must have a security leak in our branch."

DeLorean raised his hand to pause the conversation. He took a deep breath. He forgot that the identification of patients was never shared and kept strict confidence in his computer system. Less than ten people had access to these files. The breach was from outside of the network, but that did not negate the possibility the perpetrator could be from within. "You noted the breech was a week ago. Have there been any additional attempts since then?"

"We are checking a broad spectrum of dates to verify if this is a onetime incident. I will keep you posted on our findings."

DeLorean stood, walked around his desk, and patted the NCO on the back. "Good job, sergeant. Thank you for your professionalism. Let's keep this under our hats until we have all the answers, please."

The NCO nodded. "Yes. Of course."

DeLorean closed the door before returning to his chair. He took out his cell phone and placed a call.

"Hello."

"Kuka, we have a problem. Someone broke into my network and sought information from former staff members and patients on the 6th floor. Do you remember our breakfast conversation?"

"I remember. Unfortunately, I also remember I don't have clearance for this information. If that's the case, then why are you calling me? Forgive me for being terse."

DeLorean grinned. "I will tell you one thing that will grab your attention and demand your focus…not your sarcasm."

Kuka pursed her lips tightly. "Really? Ok. I'm sitting down. What will get my attention?"

"Only one patient file was read," DeLorean intentionally let the gears of curiosity spin in his sister's brain. "It was Dr. Anderson Albright's."

His ploy worked perfectly. Kuka was engrossed in what he just stated. "Albright's file was the only patient file examined?"

"That's what I said."

The air was thick with tension as silence enveloped the phone call as both considered the many possibilities of who and why these files were targeted. Kuka finally spoke. "Do you know who may have hacked in?"

"No! My team is up to their necks in data to backtrack every contact with our network, including attempted hacks. We have a lot of data to glean."

Kuka had taken another step outside of her expertise and comfort zone. The quest to find anything on Albright brought her to the limits of her emotional and psychological stability. She had never ventured into uncharted territories of this nature while meeting resistance beyond her experience. "How long do you think it will take your team to find a perpetrator?"

Even as he sat alone, DeLorean shook his head as if she could see him. "I do not know. This could take months and remain unsolved, or one of the team members could strike gold with one keystroke. It's like going through a minefield on a pogo stick…you might hit the button, but odds are you won't."

Kuka was thinking about how every resource, both human and digital, could not produce one connection to Albright. Now, her brother's network was hacked, and the files of a few employees and one patient were targeted. This was no accident or random attack. This was a well-defined, targeted breach of a specific network. Someone is familiar with the contents of these servers. But who?

Her thoughts were interrupted as DeLorean spoke. "I'll keep you posted on our progress. I know you will continue to reach out to everyone who could provide directions to Albright. We will talk more later. I must get back to work."

"I understand. Thank you."

Bobby arrived at work early. The afternoon and night of driving mindlessly disconnected him from his job, putting him behind in operations. He had a scheduled meeting to review the sector reports and another with Martinez afterward. He could answer emails and prepare questions for the early morning sector report meeting with the team. The sector meeting review went well and no concerns regarding political issues were developing or evolving today. After the meeting, his attention focused on reviewing what Martinez had discovered regarding DeLorean's network and how he should share the information regarding Chang's incident and the revelation of truth; he was still reeling from the truth.

Thirty minutes later, he broke protocol and invited Martinez to his office for a review of his off-the-radar activities. Martinez said nothing about Bobby's last order during the previous meeting regarding onsite reviews of his covert activities. Bobby invited Martinez into the office and closed the door as Martinez sat.

Bobby returned to his seat and took a deep breath. He wasn't going to talk about the black-op activities because it was used to get Martinez into his office so he could share the findings of the investigation performed by the FBI. "Chang was not the mole."

Martinez was not prepared for anything regarding Chang. He shook his head in confusion. "Excuse me. What did you say?"

"Chang was not the mole."

Martinez had not expected this statement. He sat, trying to interpret what Bobby said. "What? Chang was not the mole. What are you saying?"

Bobby crossed his arms. "Chang was innocent!"

These words made the conversation clear. "Chang wasn't the mole, and he wasn't guilty?"

"Exactly! Chang was meeting with his uncle, who had recently arrived from China and needed help finding an apartment. Chang was the uncle's banker, realtor, and immediate family member who spoke Chinese. Chang would meet him each week to help find and secure a place to live. Chang was also his banker and with Chang's death, the uncle's money will never be recovered from the bank. His uncle is like a ship without a rudder floating in the sea of life. It's so tragic and I feel it's my fault."

Martinez sat quietly for a minute. "I can't believe this. Chang was innocent the whole time?"

"Yes."

"Why would he kill himself if he were innocent? I don't understand."

"Neither do I!"

Martinez tapped his right index finger several times on the desk. "Let me recap this to ensure I understand the whole story. Each week, Chang would meet with his uncle from China to look for an apartment. Chang would put the uncle's money in his bank account to keep it secure. Chang did nothing illegal, yet he killed himself. Now the uncle has no money, no family member here who speaks Chinese, and no hope. Did I miss anything?"

"That sums it up. I'm trying to see how I can help the uncle and put the puzzle together about why Chang took his life. Hopefully, when I meet the uncle, with an interpreter, I might find some facts that are not known currently. I hate this. The mistake I made was in judgment. I messed up and because of me, Chang is dead."

"You are being too hard on yourself. I agree that this is tragic, but you must stop carrying the cross of guilt and responsibility. Other professionals reviewed the events and agreed with you that Chang needed to be questioned and arrested to stop him from being a flight risk. Yes, the arrest may have been premature or wrong, but the truth will come to light.

Chang would not hold this against you.

He was a nobleman who placed himself in a questionable situation. I understand why you feel guilty; he was a friend and confidant. You had complete trust in him until the weekly meetings. Have you considered that he should have made you aware of these meetings to avoid any misinterpretations of their purpose?"

"Not really. I've been too busy beating myself up."

"Then it's time to stop! Find a purpose in this to exonerate Chang and help his uncle. That will help you heal."

Bobby nodded in agreement. "Thank you. I'll do that."

Martinez smiled. "That's a great starting point to mend. Let's shift gears and our focus for a minute."

Bobby wasn't ready for Martinez's change of topic, but knew it was the perfect time for a mental and emotional distraction. "What's up?"

"It seems someone beat me to DeLorean's network."

This topic immediately grabbed Bobby's attention. "Somebody beat you. How?"

"Someone hacked into DeLorean's network before me. It seems we are not the only interested party in discovering the contents within his system."

Bobby stood. "That's incredible. How can that be? What are the odds of someone having the same motives as us at the same time? Hard to dismiss as coincidence."

"I'm not arguing that! What I found curious was the purpose of the hack."

Bobby looked at Martinez. "And what was that?"

Martinez had a curious expression on his face. "The uninvited guest reviewed the content of several staff members and one patient."

Bobby sat. "I'm ready. Tell me."

"The staff members were you, Marty, Angela, and Josh. The patient was Albright."

Bobby was jolted by the news that Albright's information was available and had been compromised. "How is that possible when each patient's record was uniquely identified by their room number? No names were ever used."

Martinez nodded. "That's what we were told to believe. When you think about it, patient information and identification were needed at some point to contact the family and arrange funeral accommodations. The patient information on DeLorean's network had the details no one did."

"This cannot be a shot in the dark! It had to be planned...orchestrated. The red flag in my mind is who and why? Who did this and why was it timed to happen days before you attempted to gain access?"

Martinez nodded. "I am with you on this. Something seems out of whack."

"Wait, a minute! Did you get a copy of Albright's information, or was it already removed?"

Martinez produced a manila folder accompanied by a million-dollar smile. "Look for yourself."

Bobby grabbed the folder and opened it. "Holy cow! You got it!"

Martinez laughed. "What else would you expect?"

"Forgive me for doubting you."

"You didn't doubt me, and I can't take all the credit you are throwing my way. I was surprised that Albright's information was still accessible. DeLorean's team is not expecting anyone to hack, and I believe they didn't think it could be accomplished again. Regardless, we have Albright's complete dossier."

"Complete? How do you know that?"

"Everything from day one of his hire by FDR is on those pages. My grandfather did more than James Bond. I'm serious. He was a part of so many classified and never revealed missions. I'm amazed he is still alive. By the way, there is a mention of an elixir created by a Japanese General. I think that is interesting."

In focusing on the conversation, Bobby forgot Martinez was Albright's grandson and interrogated him. "How do you know about his missions? He would never share those with you."

Martinez pursed his lips before speaking. "When I would visit his house in Norwalk, I found the trunk and notes. Over the summer of my junior-senior year, while spending time with him, I made it my quest to read every page. I was amazed."

Bobby never expected that someone, especially an immediate subordinate, would already know the contents of Albright's documents. He had made a mental note to let no topic jeopardize the revelation of specific information, especially about Albright, but it was too late. Bobby continued the conversation to see Martinez's knowledge. "Are you referring to General Ishii?"

"That's the guy. These pages are filled with incredible events hidden from the public and even our allies."

"I was told about several of your grandfather's classified endeavors when I first spoke to him."

Martinez's eyes widened. "What are you saying?"

"I spoke with him frequently when he was held on the 6th floor. It's ironic you were so close to him, yet never knew. I, too, was taken aback when your grandfather shared some of his exploits. He knew this information would be the only way I could believe and trust him. Marty and I traveled to his house in Norwalk, Iowa, which you just noted is a well-known location for you."

"If he shared the location of his home with you, that means you are a trusted part of his inner circle. Until now, Mother and I were the only people who knew about his home. Why did you go there?"

"It seems your grandfather had much more information hidden in a trunk than what DeLorean has, which you already know. Marty and I are still reviewing the content of his records for facts, activities, and covert operations."

"If you already had his information, why did you want me to hack into DeLorean's network?"

"We did not know what information about your grandfather was in the hands of the government. I could not tell you at that point. I needed your help to find his data and provide it. There may have been other sources of information unknown to us. You did an awesome job and I thank you for it. Now we can continue our quest to find out who in the government wants your grandfather's information. I need you to continue seeking answers to this question."

"I will."

"Thank you. Now let's get back to work. Remember, our next meeting will be outside of this office. I will keep you posted."

Martinez stood. "Roger that! Please excuse me." He left the office.

Bobby closed the folder and took out a fat-tipped black marker and wrote one word on the manilla folder before stowing it in a secure file cabinet. "*SKOTOS.*"

NEXT - Chapter 19

The Aristocrat sat at his desk reviewing his recent accomplishment and preparing for the next steps in his plan to gain more power. His prior mission was flawless, like all others. The return flight provided time to decompress and relax after the tense operation. He grabbed a folder from the corner of his desktop and opened it. The content was the same, but he took time to review the information for a second time to ensure he was well-versed in every detail. This would be a huge undertaking for him and his team. He could overlook nothing. This philosophy was the foundation for his success.

Nothing could be assumed or taken for granted.

He smiled as he reflected on how easily the source had surrendered the contents without hesitation. He was amazed that given the right circumstances, fear easily motivated people to go outside of their established morals and even the law. Survival became the focus of their attention, which left very little to chance; something he tried to avoid at all costs because he trusted facts over speculation.

The review of each person showed the vast difference in their ethnicity, education, interests, and philosophies. The only commonality was the location of their employment. Weaving a plan that would bring them together required careful consideration and surveillance to make sure everything would fall into place perfectly. He had never engaged in an operation of this scope and magnitude. He embraced the challenge.

William Martin was reviewing the daily reports when he suddenly looked up as if he had experienced a religious moment. The epiphany of how Sheppard enveloped his thoughts unexpectedly interrupting his routine. How could he have missed this critical piece of information? His first exchange with Sheppard was in an elevator located here. Sheppard would have credentials that allowed him access. With access, there would be a record of him entering the building. All he needed to do was review the records of who entered the building on that specific day. He sat back and smiled, hoping this would review Sheppard's identity. He picked up the desk phone and contacted security, provided the pertinent information, and would wait for the results of their investigation. He sat shaking his head in disbelief at the realization he had missed something so significant. He mentally chastised himself for failing to connect this simple search for evidence.

Sheppard was reflecting on his earlier call with Albright. The order to keep William Martin on a tight leash was moving smoothly. The morsels of information guaranteed he stayed in his lane. Albright would provide orders for the third rendezvous with Sheppard. This meeting would be the catalyst that would continue to keep Martin engaged. Sheppard returned his attention to his work.

Kuka knew DeLorean was working diligently to discover who compromised his network two weeks ago. She knew her brother would revamp the security reviews and expect daily, instead of weekly, reviews. She felt the growing frustration of failing to find anything about Albright and his documents. How could a man of Albright's scope of duties remain under the radar all these years? There had to be more about him than just his duties as an attaché to several presidents. produced answers to questions. Questions that could only be answered by accessing the files.

"Mr. President. I'm sorry for the interruption" The President spun around from looking out the window to see his Chief of Staff standing before him.

"What's up?"

"Sir, I have a very persistent man on the phone who continues to call after I told him you were busy. He continues to repeat that he knows you and needs to speak with you. He said it's very important. I think it's a prank caller just trying to say something negative to you, but in the insanity of world chaos, I could not dismiss the fact we should hear him out. Unfortunately, he refused to speak with me."

The President cleared his throat. "Very insightful. We never know what information will come across the desk and from which sources. Did our caller identify himself?"

"Yes. He said to tell you he's the tax collector."

Even though the President was immediately incensed, he acted as if it were a long-lost friend. "The Tax Collector? It's a prank all right. From a friend of mine. Please forward the call after you leave the office." He wanted to limit the number of witnesses to the call, even though a camera and audio feed were recording everything.

"Yes, sir." The Chief of Staff turned, walked out, and closed the door behind him. Seconds later, the phone rang, and the President lifted the receiver and placed it on his ear. In a muffled voice, he spoke in an angered tone. "What is your problem? I've told you never to contact me on this number. Do you have a learning disorder or are you stupid? Are you trying to get me impeached while attempting to get us both thrown in the prison?"

The evil grin appeared on the Aristocrat's face, although not seen, it visually represented the sarcastic response. "Did you just insult me? Have you lost your understanding of who is in charge? Do not push me into a corner with threats because I will retaliate, and you will be gone forever. Not as a hero, as a missing person who was the President of the United States. Do you understand me?"

The moment of boldness was brief and quickly changed to cowardice.

"Good. I made the call to show you I own everything, including you. You can never hide from me. You will always be at my beck and call if you are alive. If you want peace and semblance of freedom, which means you had better keep me happy. I reviewed the information you sent me and wanted to thank you. See, I'm not always the blood-thirsty, crazed maniacal tyrant you think I am. There is a soft side to me occasionally. Having you in my stable of political geldings is going to come in handy, very handy. I will keep you posted on what I need and when I need it. Until then, hang up, turn around, and watch the birds soar high above the cesspool of life."

Before the President could say anything, he heard the distinct click; the call was over. He placed the receiver into the cradle. His mind was in high gear as he was pushed into a position to provide classified information to a lunatic. Unfortunately, the lunatic had personal information that the President knew could never be shared with the public. The news media would destroy his career and character in seconds. He had to keep these rogue activities from his wife, too. She could not be compromised as a collaborator who knew everything about his private life. His empire would crumble, lost forever; his future, his family, his pension...everything gone! He had never betrayed his country before, but then again, some things can change your mind, like greed, fear, and intimidation. He thought, "I hope this will be over soon. I need to relax and finish my final year in the office without incident or drama." He hated the emasculated undertones that the Aristocrat implied when comparing him to one of the many geldings in his stable of politicians.

The President became incensed by the Aristocrat's arrogance and how his life was now one of servitude to the

Aristocrat. Unfortunately, the Aristocrat knew him well and held all the cards. He hung up the phone thinking that he wished he never knew about *Executive Order 13228,* which established the *Office of Homeland Security and the Homeland Security Council* per *Code of Federal Regulations* (CFR), Title 3 (2001): 796-802. He quietly watched the birds.

NICE TO MEET YOU - Chapter 20

Martin had almost completed his morning ritual of reviewing all the reports when there was a knock on the door. He looked up, surprised he did not see the face of his secretary. It was the face of someone outside of his acquaintances, which quickly became two faces of men outside his acquaintances. The men walked into his office.

The man on the left spoke first. "Do you mind if we talk to you for a few minutes?"

Martin was surprised. These men were heavy hitters, and he took no chances. His defenses were up, but he knew headquarters was a secure location. He stealthily opened the top left desk drawer, revealing his pistol. He didn't reach for it as the two gentlemen slowly sat in front of his desk. There was silence for a moment until Martin spoke. Can I ask who you are and why you just walked into my office? What did you say to my secretary?

The man on the left spoke, "Yes, we were greeted by your secretary and spoke with him. Nice young man."

The man on the right spoke. "Smart too! He listened carefully to us. Just as we expect you to do." Both men produced credentials that Martin tried to read, but they were folded and returned as quickly as displayed.

Martin stared intently into their eyes. "You don't have to intimidate me. I'm not as young and naïve as he is, and I don't intimidate easily. Let's cut to the chase. Why are you here?"

The man on the right spoke. "Why don't we do this? How about you listen carefully to our instructions? Then come with us for a little walk and we will inform you of some things along the way. How's that? If not, or you decide to put up some resistance, we will snuff you out like a bad cigarette on a hot sidewalk."

The other man spoke. "You need to slowly close the upper left drawer that has your pistol in it. We are not here to shoot or hurt you, but you're going to do everything we say."

Martin was out of his comfort zone. "Of course. I will now slowly close the drawer."

Both men nodded in agreement.

The man on the left spoke again. "It seems you have pried into areas of security that are outside of your scope of duties. A request for information was submitted by you to the *Director of Records*."

Martin immediately knew that his request for Sheppard's information had triggered this meeting. "What are you talking about?"

The man on the right spoke. "Sir, please don't play us for fools using childish responses to the issue. It will only take longer and make the meeting tense."

Martin took a deep breath. "Ok. Continue."

"You sought information regarding a person named Sheppard," as stated by the *Director of Records*. "This is an obvious violation of organizational and operational protocol, which can land you in prison."

His words were like a slap in the face. "What do you mean by a violation of organizational and operational protocol? I'm doing my job."

"Your job description does not include venturing outside of your prescribed duties to perform a rogue investigation of a highly classified individual. That decision makes a violation of national security."

Martin sat up. "How was I to know this person works in a highly classified position? If that were the case, I would have never sought assistance to identify him."

"Regardless, you went outside the boundaries, and you need to come with us."

The men arose, almost as if synchronized. The one on the left spoke, "There will be no resistance on your part...none! We will now escort you. Don't ask questions during the trip."

The man on the right spoke. "If there is resistance, you will not be happy."

Martin was angered. "Listen to me! I'm not intimidated by you, and I never will be. So cut the hero crap and get me out of here."

The man on the left spoke. "Per Mare, Per Terram."

Martin looked at him and his anger quickly subsided as he repeated the words. *"Per Mare, Per Terram."* They nodded.

"Please come with us." Even though Martin was surprised, he knew he was in the trusted company of like-minded men. These men identified their shared camaraderie from being *Royal Marine Commandos* when they said, *"Per Mare, Per Terram - By Sea, By Land."*

The man on the right spoke. "By the way, we have another issue in common."

Martin was perplexed. "And what might that me?"

The man smiled. "Dr. Anderson Albright."

Martin was surprised a second time in less than a minute. Those words consumed his complete mental processes as he entertained the possibility of meeting Albright. "Lead on gentlemen, I can't wait to see what awaits me." Perspiration formed on his forehead as he felt his hands go clammy. He was surprised at the physiological reaction when hearing Albright's name. He was humored thinking about how Pavlov's dog was conditioned for food and his reaction to Albright manifested similar reactions.

Martin walked around the desk and joined the pair. As they exited his office, he told his secretary, "Hey, I'll be back soon."

The secretary nodded as they disappeared down the corridor.

Albright wished he could be a fly on the wall when Martin was confronted with the facts. He knew Martin would be consumed with more questions while having answers that satisfied his questions about the situation. Albright smiled. Another step in his operation was complete. He was getting closer to completion.

As they walked, Shepherd knew he had played a card that brought quick attention to the dealer in this game of espionage. He hoped there would be no regrets or legal proceedings. They stopped and stood before the elevator doors. Once opened, the two escorts took Martin into the elevator. After the elevator door closed, one escort placed a key in the access hole and turned it. The top button on the elevator panel illuminated. He pressed it and the elevator rose slowly. Martin knew the key and button were for VIPs; people assigned to headquarters but who had exclusive rights in an area excluded from anyone note having an ultra-top-secret clearance. He had never been on this floor. This would be a new adventure for him. As the elevator doors opened, they were greeted at a desk by the receptionist. "Welcome gentleman."

They nodded and walked around the corner, continuing their trek down the hall. They stopped in front of a door identified as 007, which brought a smirk to Martin's face as he reflected on his identity being a product of James Bond, author, and British military officer Ian Fleming. He was intrigued. He wondered who would be the owner of office 007. The escorts knocked on the door and a voice invited them in. They walked over and stood in front of the desk. The person behind the desk had his back to them. The chair turned, and a man stood. Martin looked eye to eye with someone he didn't recognize. The man extended his hand and said, "William Martin, nice to meet you, face-to-face."

Martin immediately knew that voice and mannerisms. It was Shepard. "Nice of you to stop by."

Martin smiled. "It wasn't as if I had a choice. It seems every time I meet you, there is a twist in proper etiquette and protocol."

Sheppard laughed. "True, but you must admit, I introduced you to some delicious fish and chips!"

Martin nodded. "You did that. Thank you, my good man."

"Now that you have officially met me, let's talk about Albright."

Martin was immediately engaged. "Thank you. I've been seeking answers to many questions about Dr. Albright."

"Before we continue, please allow me to convey his thanks to you."

Martin was surprised again. "Excuse me? Dr. Albright told you to thank me on his behalf?"

"Yes, he did. We put you on a chase to find out why Churchill and Albright met before Churchill was even Prime Minister. You were used to reveal a communist agent who had been tailing you for several months. We knew there was no documentation regarding President Wilson, Albright, and Churchill. However, your passion to find answers and meet with Sheppard at the restaurant bar revealed the person tailing you. He was arrested without incident. For this, Dr. Albright thanks you. I was the one who rewarded you with the free lunch."

Martin was beside himself. In less than thirty minutes, he experienced more ups and downs than a person riding a roller coaster.

"Do you have questions for me now that we have met?"

Martin slid forward in the chair. "Who are you?"

Sheppard grinned. "Someone you would have never expected. I am the Director of International Security for the United States with the UK. This is an ultra-top-secret position that provided me access to meet you in the elevator the first day and monitor your activities since. Dr. Albright has been a part of secret operations for decades as the attaché of several presidents. He was the key to opening doors and placing me in this position. I, too, am an attaché to the President, but in another capacity. Your access and responsibility to review daily security reports captured the attention of a communist regime, which I cannot name, who placed a tail on you. Even though your information was intact here, we could not take the risk of having you abducted and subjected to harsh persuasion techniques for them to get information. When you met me at the restaurant, the first time we had leaked false information to the spy, hoping he would monitor your meeting with a spy while at the park. It worked. He took the bait, and you got a meal."

"I feel so special knowing that I was the bait. I'm glad I didn't get abducted and tortured. I'm not good at waterboarding. What's next?"

"You will continue your duties helping the Spanish liaison and reviewing your reports." Sheppard had to keep Martin in the loop, so Bobby continued access to their network.

"I understand."

"Thank you, Martin. We appreciate your services. What's the name of the Spanish liaison?"

"Colonel Roberto Arrollos. He is highly intelligent and engaged. I will reach out to him this week to see if he needs anything."

"Excellent! Thank you for your continued dedication to service and unparalleled passion for recognition." Sheppard stood and extended his hand.

Martin stood and shook hands. "Nice to finally meet you."

"Likewise. Have a wonderful day and know I will be in touch periodically."

"Yes, sir."

Martin and the escorts left, but before exiting, he turned and exclaimed. "What about the meeting with Churchill and Albright I was searching for? Why did they meet?"

> *Sheppard smiled. "They met, so you would meet me today."*

Martin's expression was confusion. Then reality manifested itself now. "There never was a meeting! You used me to get the spy! I wasted so much time searching for nothing!"

Sheppard shook his head 'No.' "You were an asset. Just like your namesake, William Martin. Now you know how the Germans felt when they realized the truth!"

Martin was not humored by Sheppard's use of history to answer the question. "Thanks a lot. I'm not happy, but at least I contributed to the mission!"

"Yes, you did! Thank you. I kept my word. At the restaurant, I promised I would provide the answer regarding the meeting, and I kept my word!" Martin and the escorts left the office. Sheppard picked up his cell phone and made a call, which was immediately answered. "Everything went well. Better than expected. He didn't sense anything out of the ordinary. Bobby will hear from him. His gateway to the network will be invaluable and continue. Yes, sir. Thank you." Sheppard hung up and laughed as he thought about the expression on Martin's face when he realized he was used. He thought, "Life is a series of events, some good, some bad, but in the end, it doesn't matter!"

Albright sat back in his chair, smiling. Bobby was given *Carte Blanche* to the network. The mission would continue as planned.

SUPRISE - Chapter 21

The Aristocrat closed the folder in frustration, and then immediately reopened it. This time, he removed all the pages and aligned them in order from left to right on his desk. He stared at each page; it seemed everything he needed was there, except one item, and that item became the focus of his attention...which would soon become an obsession. He needed this item; however, his resources were limited. Limited resources would not stop him; they would not impede his desire to make the mission succeed. The man had money. He had the determination, and he had the wherewithal to find the missing item. He summoned his commander and four captains for an impromptu meeting. They would arrive in less than 30 minutes.

Marty and Dr. Martinez had been working throughout the morning. Dr. Martinez came to Marty. "Are you as hungry as me?"

Marty responded, "Famished!" Then laughed.

Dr. Martinez laughed with her. "Yes, I'm famished too!"

Marty smiled. "If you are inviting me to eat, I was ready an hour ago!"

Dr. Martinez nodded in agreement. "Then we need to take a break and get out of the *Smithsonian*."

Marty was surprised. "Out? These are the words from the woman who never leaves to eat! Are you saying the kitchenette will not meet your culinary and epicurean needs today?"

Dr. Martinez nodded. "Definitely! Let's stretch our legs, get some fresh air, and find a place to eat."

"Lead on doctor!"

They grabbed their purses and headed out the door.

Dr. Martinez opened the door and Marty passed through, thanking her. "Marty, I have not eaten in this area for years. Have you gone anywhere nearby?"

"Yes, Bobby and I found a very quaint sandwich shop near to here. The food and service were outstanding. Are you up for a sandwich?"

"That sounds perfect. Lead the way." They chit-chatted about the news and issues each faced in and out of the office. This venture would provide a much-needed mental break from the office. As they arrived, Marty shared how they were greeted, seated, and served by a bubbly waitress from Finland. Marty also added that the prices were very competitive. As they entered, they were greeted by the waitress assigned per protocol: greet, seat, and serve. These three assignments ensured the customer-server experience began at the front door and continued until they departed. The server asked them to follow her to the table, provided menus, and quickly served water from a busboy.

Dr. Martinez smiled. "For a small establishment, they are prepared to provide excellent service, which assures customers they are valued. I'm impressed!"

Marty opened the menu, and Dr. Martinez followed. "So, what does a world-renowned history expert eat when she sneaks out of the office?"

"Anything I'm in the mood for and today I can eat anything!" They laughed and then put their attention on the menu before the server returned. Standing across the room surveying her customers, Kiki, DeLorean's niece, noticed Marty sitting at a table with another woman. She was almost positive she had met her before, but she didn't see Bobby, which made her doubt Marty was the woman in the photographs on her uncle's desk. As she tended to her customers, she had the opportunity to get closer to the table. As she passed, Marty made eye contact and pointed at her. "Hey, I remember you. The student from Finland."

Kiki smiled. "Yes! I saw you, but I wasn't sure if I should approach."

"Nonsense! How have you been? How is school?"

Kiki was surprised by the series of questions. "I'm well, thank you."

Marty extended her hand toward Dr. Martinez. "Let me introduce you to one of the most incredible historians on the face of the earth. My friend, Dr. Martinez."

Kiki smiled. "Nice to meet you, Dr. Martinez."

"My pleasure. Nice to meet you too."

"So, you are a history buff?"

Marty laughed. "She is more than that! They have her overseeing all the antiquities and archiving their geographical origins at the *Smithsonian*. We work together."

Dr. Martinez smiled. "Yes, I have an extensive background in finding old things. I guess me being old adds to my awareness."

They all laughed.

Kiki touched Dr. Martinez's shoulder. "You are not that old, and I am impressed. I've met no one who is an expert in history and antiquities. Please excuse me. I need to get to my customers. Nice to see you again and nice to have met you, Dr. Martinez."

Kiki nodded and walked away.

"She seems like an amiable person."

Marty nodded. "She is. We had a delightful time visiting when she served us. I can't imagine leaving my home country and family to attend classes while working and having to speak a second language. That is a tall order for domestic students who speak English and live minutes away."

The waitress came to the table and took their order. Minutes later, the food was set before them, and their attention was redirected to the delicious sandwiches and sides.

Between bites, Dr. Martinez spoke. "I find it interesting that a young woman from Finland would be in DC working at a restaurant while she attended college. That requires time and dedication."

Marty dabbed her lips with a napkin. "She had mentioned she has relatives who live and work in the DC area. I'm sure their support is priceless."

Kiki walked to the back and quickly texted DeLorean. She informed him that the woman she saw in the photograph on his desk had returned. DeLorean texted, "Keep an eye on her. I will be there shortly." DeLorean's frustration overflowed as he chastised her in a text message. "Why didn't you let me know sooner? You know we were looking for that woman." He immediately left the office and texted Kuka as he walked to the car. She responded that she, too, was en route to the restaurant. DeLorean voice-texted Kiki, "How long have they been there?"

Kiki responded. "They've been there for almost a half-hour." She felt bad he chastised her, especially after being told the man and woman were dead. How was she to know the woman could be alive? She discovered this today after making direct contact. She shook her head in frustration. Her father was never happy unless he was unhappy.

DeLorean cursed under his breath as he negotiated in and out of the slow-moving downtown Washington, DC traffic, fearing that he would miss the opportunity to see if Marty was alive. Fortunately for him, he could park near the restaurant and quickly make his way through the front door. Kiki saw him and pointed out the table where Marty and Dr. Martinez were seated. DeLorean immediately stepped aside so he wouldn't be recognized, then took a couple of pictures with his cell phone and forwarded them to his sister. The black widow jumped on it. She agreed it was Marty and told him to stay back and follow her to where she worked. DeLorean texted Kuka and told Kiki he would stay and wait for them to leave.

Kiki whispered to DeLorean that Marty had mentioned they worked together at the *Smithsonian* and Dr. Martinez was the curator of history and antiquities. DeLorean was enthralled.

The Smithsonian was only a few blocks away, and he felt his heart leap.

He would tail the ladies as they returned to work. If everything went as planned, he knew there was the possibility Bobby wasn't too far away. His thoughts were interrupted as the text from Kuka informed him she had parked and was headed toward the restaurant. He texted her and told her to position herself somewhere along the return route to the *Smithsonian*. They waited until the ladies left the restaurant and stealthily followed them on their return trek to their office. DeLorean and Kuka now had the information necessary to monitor Marty, while hoping Bobby would eventually show up. After gathering all the information required to track them and establish future points for observation, they returned to the restaurant. During the meal, they took time to eat and review the various options to follow Marty, which could be the yellow-brick road to Bobby and Albright. They kept their fingers crossed.

The phone on his desk rang, and he pressed the intercom button. "Yes."

"Sir, the commander and captains have arrived. Shall I send them in?"

"No, take them to the conference room. I will meet them shortly." He shifted in his seat and gathered the five packets of documents prepared to share with them.

"Yes, sir."

He looked around the room. An involuntary movement he did whenever he was stressed. Minutes later, he stood, took the packets in hand, and exited the office to his rendezvous with the five leaders. As he entered the room, the men stood in respect as the commander greeted him. The Aristocrat nodded in approval, then the men sat. He looked at each man seated before him searching for fear or reservations; either of which could compromise the mission. Everyone seemed comfortable. He slid each packet across the table to the person sitting before him. He opened his file and began speaking. "Captains, before you are the individual team assignments, you and your A-team will perform under the oversight and operational directives of our commander. There will be no failure because there is no room for errors or misjudgments in your mission. These are the most critical undertakings ever performed by our organization. The operations will begin at precisely the same time and are executed most expeditiously. Your return orders and assignments have been noted. Please review these orders completely. I will return in thirty minutes to answer questions." The Aristocrat left the room.

Bobby sat with the team and began the daily review of the sector activities. Everything was routine until Gold began sharing the information he had recently gathered. Sir, there has been an enormous increase in communication exchanges in Germany on landlines, cellular phones, and emails. It seems several factions of Q-anon and Antifa sympathizers are sharing information and possibly planning something. This information has also been discovered by other domestic agencies outside of our department.

"Any ideas of what this shows?"

"Not yet! I'm keeping close attention to this."

Bobby acknowledged Gold's pledge to continue monitoring the situation. "Does anyone have anything to add to this German situation?" They exchanged glances and in unison shook their heads 'no.'

Bobby looked around the room. "Keep your eyes open for activity in your sectors. Just because we have movement in Germany, it doesn't mean it won't cross into other areas of Europe. Is that clear?"

"Yes, sir!"

"Thanks, team. You are highly trained and appreciated. Dismissed."

Bobby returned to his office and began reviewing the information Gold had already forwarded to him.

DeLorean was reviewing the world activity report sent from his NCOIC. There was an alert specific to increases in communication exchanges in Germany on landlines, cellular phones, and emails. The notation failed to mention or speculate why the increases had recently occurred, but prompted security operations to look closely at the area each day. DeLorean sat back in his chair and began scribbling on a notepad. He was oblivious that Kuka was standing in the doorway.

Bobby was reviewing the reports, especially what was happening in Germany. He was interrupted by a knock on the door. He looked up to see Sgt. Martinez was standing there. Bobby responded, "What's going on?"

Martinez smiled. "I can't believe it. My mom lives in that office and never gets out. Today, or whatever reason, she called me all excited about how she and Marty had gone to this little restaurant that specialized in sandwiches and sides."

Bobby smiled. "That place has delicious sandwiches!"

Sgt. Martinez questioned him, "So, you've been there before?"

Bobby nodded. "Yes, it was delicious. Marty and I took a break one day and strolled past it. The smell of fresh bread filled our nostrils, and we couldn't resist trying their food."

Martinez smiled. "No wonder Mom was excited."

Bobby stood. "Let's go!"

Martinez looked puzzled. "Go? Where?"

Bobby's head motioned to the hall. "How about we take a break and get out of here? I'm tired of looking at reports, walls, and these ugly faces. I need a break. Are you up for one too?"

Martinez laughed. "Sure. Sounds like a plan to me, which will also give us some time to review my progress on my other assignment."

"Great idea. I'll drive." Both men exited the office and, in less than twenty minutes, arrived. They parked a vehicle and headed to the front door of the restaurant and walked in. They were greeted by a hostess, who told them a table would be ready in just a minute.

Bobby looked around the room and froze.

He grabbed Martinez by the shoulders and spun around so his back was to the crowd. Martinez saw the stunned expression on his face. "Is everything okay, Colonel?" Martinez kept with the protocol. Bobby looked him directly in the eyes. "I want you to look over my left shoulder and describe the officer in uniform and the woman with him."

Martinez was expressionless and crept his head left so he could see around Bobby. "Ok. The officer is wearing a khakis uniform, and the woman is wearing a white blouse covered by black blazer and matching slacks."

"Is she armed?"

This question caught Martinez off guard. He scanned her blazer for any indicators she was wearing a shoulder holster. Nothing. He scanned her beltline...nothing, but when he scanned her legs, he could see the faint outline of something in the right ankle area. "Looks like she has a compact pistol on the right ankle."

"What are they doing?"

"Standing. It looks as if they are waiting for the waitress to bring the bill. The waitress just walked up, and they are exchanging hugs. I don't think that is a common protocol for thanking customers. They seem to know each other."

Bobby nodded. "Probably. The officer is LTC DeLorean, the officer I replaced on the 6th floor."

Martinez had heard that name before. "Isn't he the person who knew the purpose of the 6th floor?"

"Yes. He was promoted and transferred after a female patient went crazy one day. He arranged her relocation, if they let her live, and denied everything later when the Senate began an investigation after Albright disappeared and they closed 6th-floor operations."

Martinez scowled. "That man cannot be trusted."

The hostess arrived and escorted them to a table away from the door. This was perfect because their backs were to DeLorean, the woman, and the waitress as they were seated, and the others walked toward the exit. Bobby watched as they shared hugs again before walking out. The waitress returned to tending to her customers while DeLorean and Kuka disappeared.

Bobby's mind was in high gear. "We need to find out who that woman is. If she is packing heat, then she is not a typical date. If she is with him, she could be CIA or NSA. I need you to help find out. Before continuing, let me ask, does she look familiar to you?"

"No. What do you need from me?"

"I'm going to the restroom. This will allow you to flag down their waitress and ask her about today's special. After getting her into a conversation, see what you can find out about the people she was with."

"Roger that! I'll text you when I finish."

Bobby grinned. "Sounds great." He stood and walked to the restroom.

Martinez scanned to the room and spotted Kiki. He gave her a wave and motioned her to the table.

"Yes, sir. How can I help you?"

"As I was waiting for a table, I saw you hugging some customers. How do I get a hug?"

Kiki laughed. "We don't give hugs. That is my father who works in the Army and his sister who is visiting, working, here from Finland."

"That's a nice way to have a reunion and share your love."

Kiki slightly lowered her head. "I'm trying to make up with them. They were mad at me earlier because of something I did."

Martinez put on an expression of genuine concern. "How can anyone be mad at a beautiful woman like you? What could you have possibly done to make them angry?"

Kiki blushed. "A few weeks ago, I was having dinner with dad and my aunt Kuku when I saw some photographs on his desk. The people looked familiar. I told them I thought the man and the woman in the photos had eaten here before. He practically went crazy and yelled at me for looking at anything on his desk. He works on some secret stuff for the military and told me to never, regardless of the situation, look at anything on his desk."

Martinez fished for more information. "He shouldn't have gotten angry if the photos were on his desk for anyone to see."

She smiled. "That's exactly what I thought! He started saying something about them being dead and that I shouldn't say anything about them. Well, today the woman was here with her friend or boss, so I called my dad. He was here in minutes, watching the women and taking notes. He followed them to where they worked, then returned with his sister. They had lunch but only spoke about some papers, the woman in the photo, more papers, and wondered where the man from the other photo could be. I felt invisible."

"No one as beautiful as you could ever be invisible."

She smiled again. "Thank you. You are so kind."

Martinez smiled. "You said your aunt is here from Finland working?"

"Yes. She has an office at the *Finnish Embassy* but is never there. She also has a secret job like her dad did and is always traveling around the world looking for people. What do you do?"

"I'm in the Army. I'm here helping a buddy of mine and we stopped by to get a sandwich. I heard the food was great and a beautiful woman was working here."

Kiki blushed and looked around the room. "Too bad for you. She didn't come to work today."

Martinez smiled. "I think you are mistaken. Please allow me to correct you. She is standing in front of me."

Kiki looked at him without saying a word.

"What happened? Did I say something wrong?"

"No. I haven't had anyone say such nice things to me."

"I'm only telling you the truth. Do you have a man in your life?"

Kiki was surprised at his directness. "Uhhhmm…no. Why?"

"I was hoping to see if you might go out to eat or check out a movie with me sometime."

"I'm working here and attending college courses. I don't have much time, but I'll see."

Martinez smiled. "That means you are spending too much time keeping busy. You will need a break from time to time. What do you think? Will you give me a chance to free you from work and school?"

"How will I contact you?"

"We need to exchange telephone numbers. Can I have your number, please? Then I will text you mine."

Kiki hesitated for a moment but knew a man in the Army should be safe. She shared her number. "I've got to get back to work. Thank you. Call me Saturday after 12."

"I will. Take care." He had a huge smile on his face. He texted Bobby, then Kiki.

Before stepping out of the hallway, Bobby scanned the dining area for any familiar faces or anyone watching him. All clear. He returned to the table and sat. Martinez had a smile on his face that did not reflect seriousness. "What's up with you? Why the big smile?"

"I got you some very interesting info and a potential date?"

"What? You were supposed to get information, not set up a situation where you become friends with the enemy."

"She isn't the enemy. Are you going to focus on the information or my dating life?"

Bobby glared are Martinez. "Continue if you can, Casanova!"

Martinez laughed, then his expression when serious. "We have a problem."

Bobby leaned in. "What type of problem?"

Martinez glanced over his left and right shoulders. "DeLorean knows that Marty is alive and where she works."

Bobby's lips pursed. "How did that happen?"

"Remember the waitress you met on your last visit? Well, DeLorean is her father."

Bobby interrupted. "You must be kidding me! What the heck! Of all the people in the world, Marty and I meet her. And you asked her out on a date? Are you stupid?"

Martinez wasn't humored. "DeLorean hasn't a clue of who I am. If I go on a date with her, there is the possibility we will end up at daddy's apartment where he keeps his classified documents in plain view on his desk. Now do you understand?"

Bobby nodded. "How do you know his office has classified documents?"

"That's why DeLorean is here. Now I will share the meat of our problem. It seems our waitress called daddy."

Bobby frowned. "How do you know that?"

"She told me that her father and aunt had invited her to dinner a few weeks ago and during the visit, she saw photos of you and Marty on his desk. She told him she had seen you both at the restaurant. An argument ensued in which he told her you both were dead, she was mistaken, and to never look at anything on his desk."

Bobby felt his stomach tighten.

"It seems her father scolded her for looking at things on his desk because they were secret. However, today, Marty and mom came here to eat. Marty recognized her, got her attention, introduced mom, and told her they worked at the *Smithsonian*."

Bobby became angry. "What else?"

"The icing on the cake was Marty reaching out to her, which, in no uncertain terms, verified that Kiki was correct and positively identified Marty. To save face and prove she knew what she was talking about, she called daddy and told him that Marty was here. He headed over as quickly as possible and just walked out of here."

Bobby sat, emotionless. His fists clenched tighter. "Well...we need a plan. I know DeLorean and he will monitor Marty's every move. This means you will go to the motel immediately and get my stuff because I need to move. We will use Marty to bring him, DeLorean, into our web."

Martinez grinned. "I am going to assume that this part of our plan will not be shared with Marty."

"Exactly! The less she knows, the better. If she is taken hostage and tortured, I will remain hidden."

"What a lovely purpose for your actions...self-preservation!"

Bobby quickly made eye contact. "That's not what I meant, and you know it. Stop messing with me! This is serious and you know we cannot compromise the mission regardless of the losses."

Martinez asked, "What about the woman who is with DeLorean?"

Bobby smiled and raised his eyebrows. "Well, Casanova, it looks like you had better get some answers from your date."

Their conversation was interrupted by a waitress who took their order. After eating, Bobby went to pay the bill as Martinez quickly made his way to Kiki and verified the phone date on Saturday. Everything was a go. As they walked to the car, Bobby handed Martinez the key to his room. "I'll take a cab back. Please get everything from the room, return the key, and check me out. Remember, I'm Roberto Arrollos."

"Yes, sir. When I finish, I'll call you to see where we will meet and where you will be staying."

"Thank you. I'll have a new location by then. I appreciate your help. See you soon." Martinez continued to the vehicle as Bobby called a cab. As Bobby waited for the cab, he texted Albright and warned him the location had been compromised. Albright responded, "I'll take care of everything." Bobby stared at the screen and reread the message, thinking "What will Albright do next?"

PLANS - Chapter 22

As DeLorean drove away, he was consumed with finding Bobby and Albright. He ran several surveillance scenarios in his mind. The operation, regardless of the protocol, would have to be invisible; a black operation with no one outside of this team knowing. He would schedule an impromptu meeting with his team immediately when he arrived. This would be the culmination of his career when he found Bobby, Albright, and the documents. He smiled. He would arrive at the office 20 minutes later.

Kuka shared the same concerns and considerations as her brother. She knew his modus operandi with his team, and she would bring peripheral support that would encapsulate the operation and form a dragnet of observation. After several weeks of failed leads, she felt the exhilaration of being back in the game and would contact her resources. She was the hunter.

The Aristocrat introduced the goals and expectations of the operation. He stood and walked to the wall monitor as the steps were detailed and images of the immediate areas for each were displayed to ensure strict situational awareness. The four teams would be deployed to different areas for their mission to locate and secure a soft target. The details of each operation showed similar steps, but the locations and details of each required precision execution and knowledge of the area. The results were the same...each soft target would be removed at precisely the same time and secured for future use. After making the presentation, some team members shared questions and concerns.

> *Each topic was addressed, ensuring nothing could go wrong.*

Once he was satisfied the plans were understood, he dismissed all personnel except the Commander. Before sitting, the Aristocrat walked into his private vault and returned with two brandy snifters and a bottle of *Hennessy Paradis Rare Cognac*, typically valued at $1,300.00 per bottle. The Aristocrat placed the snifters on the desk, opened the bottle, and poured a portion larger than normal into each glass. He placed the bottle down and took a snifter in each hand. He extended a snifter to the Commander who stood. "To our success, sir!" They shared the toast as the glass met, making the distinctive sound only produced by the finest of crystal. The men took the sip, then sat. The operation was officially in motion.

Albright placed the phone on the desk. The information Bobby provided was concerning, but nothing to panic about. One thing he had learned in life was any situation, regardless of how critical, had a solution. He smiled and picked up the phone. In a minute, he was talking with the solution - person.

Martinez quickly gathered everything in the room, including a couple of towels, which were in a heap of clothing to be washed by hospitality. He packed everything he could into the suitcases and hung everything from the closet on the guest cart rail. The cart was full of everything because Martinez wanted to make one trip. Less than ten minutes later, the cart was empty, and the back seat and trunk were full. He took the cart and card keys to the lobby, checked out, and got a receipt. After thanking the receptionist, he disappeared and called Bobby. He needed the rendezvous point. While Martinez was gathering his personal effects, Bobby had already made reservations at a nearby hotel and texted the information to Martinez. Bobby couldn't leave Marty without his security, and the five-minute drive from the new location was acceptable. Marty would be informed of his relocation before the end of her workday, but not the location or what caused the change. If she knew she was the bait to draw DeLorean and Kuka into her world, things wouldn't be pleasant. Bobby returned to his review of the surveillance information. The afternoon passed quickly. After Martinez performed the housekeeping chores for Bobby, he stayed in the room and watch sports until Bobby arrived. He felt this was deserved because domestic engineering was outside of his job description. He sank into the plush recliner and was oblivious to the sports as sleep quickly numbed his senses. Two hours later, knocking on the door would awaken him.

MISSING - Chapter 23

As DeLorean drove away, he was consumed with excitement that Marty was alive. His focus was now directed on finding Bobby and Albright. While driving home, he called Kuka and presented several surveillance options. After some in-depth discussion, they agreed to take the mission upon themselves. The fewer people who knew about it, the more secure it would be. DeLorean arrived home with an energy he hadn't experienced in the months since Albright disappeared and, unfortunately, his team was terminated with extreme prejudice by Bobby. This was rare, and he was going to embrace the moment and relax. He took a shower, put on shorts, a T-shirt, and tennis shoes, then sat on the couch. The stillness was boring. He grabbed the stereo remote and turned on some relaxing music. He then took his tablet and began reading the news. He discovered some news agencies provided credible information that helped him and his team by providing direction and insight into world controversy. While other sources were nothing more than misinformation, lies, and conjecture. After 20 minutes, he got up to get something to drink and complement it with a protein cookie, which would hold off his hunger pangs while he reviewed the information at his desk. Walking to this bedroom, he sipped his drink and took small bites from the cookie to avoid spreading a path of crumbs from the kitchen. He loved the spacious bedroom. It provided a sense of freedom from the confines of his small military office. He sat in the soft high-back-office chair, then rolled to the desk. He would review the file containing information about Albright and photographs of Bobby and Marty.

He reached for the folder. It wasn't there.

He sat back, confused for the moment because he remembered the file was atop his disk when Kiki looked at the photographs. The file was no longer on top of his desk. He looked through the desk drawers...nothing. He stood and walked around the bedroom, looking for the file. Nothing. The folder was missing. He returned to the chair, sat, and opened his briefcase. No folder. Something wasn't right. He didn't misplace the folder. He was meticulous about keeping the files organized and secure. He picked up the phone and called Kuka. After explaining the situation to her, she said she'd be right over. He heard the concern in her voice. He looked around the room, wondering what had happened to the folder.

The silence was broken as the radio crackled. "Target two has arrived. All stations stand by. Falcon, do you have eyes on the target?"

"Yes, Condor. Falcon is monitoring target two movements. Will advise when they enter the nest (area of operation)."

Condor watched through thermal imaging binoculars. "I have a heat signature on target one. Currently stationary."

"This is Falcon. Target two has arrived and is headed to the nest. No signs of weapons. ETA is less than one minute."

Condor watched target number two enter the building. "Hawk. Target two is headed to the nest."

Hawk pointed to each member. Using hand signals, each team member nodded in agreement and activated their night vision goggles, and secured their weapons. They were ready for their arrival. Target two arrived at the door and knocked.

"Target one is on site. Kill the lights in five seconds." Target one opened the door. Just as target two was stepping forward, the lights went out. The team emerged silently from the adjacent room, the building's central air conditioning center. In complete darkness, the two unsuspecting people were aggressively pushed to the floor. Both landed hard on the floor and were stunned. In seconds, their hands were forced behind their backs, wrists flex-cuffed, tape placed over their mouths, and a black hood pulled over their head. They were lifted by their arms and pushed onto the couch. The door was closed, and the lights turned on.

"As professionals, I'm sure you both are aware that you have been taken hostage. I also trust that you will do everything I say if you want to stay alive. Please nod your heads if you understand." Each nodded their head. Their chests heaved as the pressure of sensory deprivation crept into their minds, stoking their fears.

You will go with us, and should you decide to struggle, run, or make noise, I will take aggressive actions to immobilize you. Please do as I say because once I serve pain, I will continue administering it. The masks moved inward and outward as the targets struggled to breathe, hoping to reduce their anxiety as they assessed the situation.

Hawk spoke into this microphone. "The packages are secure and ready for delivery."

"Roger that. Transportation is standing by."

Hawk nodded at the team. They grabbed each target by their arms and pulled them to their feet. Moving silently, they took the stairs as the targets stumbled and were dragged down the remaining floors. They exited the building, a black van arrived, and the cargo door slid open. Everyone quickly entered the van. It disappeared into the darkness.

Condor watched from a distance and placed a call using a cell phone. "The packages are on the move and will arrive shortly." The call was to the point. Condor returned to his vehicle and drove to the predesignated rendezvous.

Even though the knock at the door was expected, it briefly startled DeLorean as it broke his concentration. He got up from the chair and opened the door. He was met by a serious expression on his sister's face.

"Nice to see you with such a warm smile."

She pushed him aside as she stepped inside. "I'm very concerned with what you told me. Please fill in the details. I hate suspense unless I'm the person causing it."

DeLorean closed the door and returned to the bedroom with Kuka close behind. They sat as he spoke. "I haven't sat at the desk for a couple of days, which doesn't help, but someone has obviously gained entrance and taken the folder. I cannot say the folder was the only information compromised, but it is the most important document in my possession. I mean, that I had in my possession."

Kuka interrupted. "This is not good! Not only has the folder been compromised, but so have we, and you know how much I hate looking over my shoulder whenever we have integrity issues. So, what are your thoughts? Do you have a plan?"

"The folder may not be as important as we once thought. With the discovery of Marty and her work location, the contents of our folder are coming to light; text and images have been replaced with tangible data sources."

In less than one minute, Kuka was brought up to speed. Unfortunately, there was no plan in place to locate the folder and the person or persons who took it. "Do you think this has anything to do with us finding Marty?"

"How could that be possible? No one knows anything about our knowledge of Nurse Bell." The two operators stationed outside in a mini cargo van looked at each other, smiled, and gave a high-five; the listening devices worked perfectly.

"Brother, you know that arrogance is a weapon the enemy can use to capitalize on you. It's jeopardized you in the past and I ask that you keep it in cheque until we have everything we need. Told him to fill her in on the details. It only took him 30 seconds as he explained the folder was gone, how he checked everything, looked everywhere, and yet it was not there. Kuka was concerned the folder that contained everything imaginable regarding Bobby and Albright was somewhere in the world. She wasn't happy. Someone intentionally took the folder. Unfortunately, her comfort in this situation was inconsequential. During the next hour, they reconsidered the use of DeLorean's goons to provide surveillance, which would help them maintain a low profile. The missing folder sent an obvious message that nothing or anyone was secure. Kuka stayed the night with her brother. She had to avoid isolation and vulnerability.

After a few hours of drinking, the bottle was empty, and the men were down to their last glass of cognac. The Aristocrat smiled at his counterpart. "Americans are so arrogant. Unfortunately, their arrogance blinds them to the truth of who is running the world and in charge. When America became oil dependent and relied on foreign countries to provide their insatiable thirst for gas-guzzling automobiles, they surrendered their security. This became the first key to owning Americans. Now, years later, they have outsourced most of their technology and industry to China to save a nickel. How ignorant. President Clinton's decision to let China purchase IBM's microcomputer division, big blue, became big red and now China holds the keys to strangling America in every arena of natural resources, manufacturing, and technology."

The Commander smiled. "Sir, I don't think China matters."

The Aristocrat was surprised. Even in a state of drunkenness, the Commander's words grabbed his attention. "How can you even suggest such a crazy notion?"

"Americans are their own worst enemies. They use social media and news outlets as political tools to promote and cause division. The once 'United States' has become divided. The fragmentation of their culture and dedication to each other is a thing of the past as they fight because of color, religion, gender, abortion, slavery, greed, and sexual identity. They are indoctrinating themselves into oblivion. The Chinese sit back, quietly watching, then when the time is right they will invade Taiwan and the computer chip industry, and its secrets will belong to China. Weak

American Presidents squandered everything, including their power, for money and fame. The fear and respect America once heralded before the world is a thing of the past and the irony is that the woke mentality will erase it from the history books. By the second generation of the woke movement will have erased any remnants of their past greatness, all forgotten. The mighty eagle is nothing more than a foreign-dependent chicken fit for slaughter."

An evil grin formed on the Aristocrat's face. "You are a genius! That is so true! America will become a third-world country because they have allowed themselves to be controlled by other nations and selfish interests. They would sell their mother for a dime if they thought it would make them rich. They live in denial. Our only concern should be Israel. Let us celebrate our hidden victories as we prepare for our next triumph." The Aristocrat raised his glass as the Commander joined the toast of their modest celebration and future victory. The Commander received a text, "Phase One complete."

He raised his glass. "I propose another toast. Phase One complete."

The Aristocrat raised his glass. "To Phase One and our victory!"

Bobby was in deep conversation with Marty regarding his move without providing her any thoughts of his intentions and location. He took the time to explain his motivations, intentions, and results. She was not amused at being the bait to reveal DeLorean, his sister, and their intentions. Bobby assured her everything would be fine, but until then, they would be limited to contact via telephone, text, and email only. Another reason is she became increasingly angry.

Bobby tried to calm her. "Marty, you need to look at the situation outside of your box. This is larger than we ever imagined, and Albright is aware of what is happening. In fact, he told me that every problem has a solution. I interpret that as his way of saying he is involved. However, we will know nothing until it happens. That's his modus operandi."

"I understand, however, I don't want to be in limbo for who knows how long. Why don't we create a scenario that will bring DeLorean and his sister out of hiding quickly?"

"That's a great idea. Unfortunately, we must wait for Albright before we take any action against DeLorean. You know the rules."

"I know the rules, I don't like the rules, and I don't want to play by them!"

Before Bobby could say another word, he received a text from Albright. "Relax. On it. Talk soon."

"I just received a text from Albright. Relax. On it. Talk soon."

Bobby could hear Marty's frustration as she spoke. "Relax. On it. Talk soon. What kind of plan is that? He should have said, 'See you when I'm good and ready.' What type of leadership is that? Let's wait forever or when I contact you again."

"You need to stop being a drama queen! I don't know why you are so frustrated, but help us get DeLorean, please. Now get some rest and we will talk tomorrow."

Marty rolled her eyes. "Easy for you to say. You are not alone in this world. Good night." With that, she disconnected and prepared for bed.

Bobby knew she was upset and alone. He would have to keep in close contact with her. He would also advise Albright and suggest Dr. Martinez keep in closer contact with Marty. He sat back and realized just how tired he was. He went to bed. Sleep would be a wonderful friend.

AWAKENING – Chapter 24

The aristocrat awoke with a pounding headache. He knew he had ventured outside of the professional boundaries he set for his physical, emotional, intellectual, and leadership limitations. He sat on the edge of the bed with his head in his hands and silently scolded himself for allowing a moment of drinking to dictate his actions and jeopardize the availability of the chain of command. He was reckless and needed to stay away from the paltry endeavors and imbibing of the ignorant as they routinely threw their lives away. He was above that and his ego and narcissistic drive that would never allow this moment to be repeated. If anything had gone south, the team would have been left in the dark and the mission compromised. Fortunately, they performed perfectly and executed the operation without issues. Phase One was complete and the operations for Phase Two, Phase Three, and Phase Four were now in motion.

Before the morning briefing, Bobby asked to speak with Martinez. After their common salutations, Bobby asked, "How is your progress on the DeLorean network?"

"Still haven't cracked the code, but it shouldn't be much longer."

Bobby nodded. "I think, actually I'm hoping, that DeLorean will direct his attention to following Marty and your mother and also direct his team's attention to gathering information about their activities, which could help you slide under the radar."

Martinez smiled. "Without knowing him, I do not know what to expect."

Bobby grinned. "I know him well, and his ego will motivate his attention. He will have every resource focused on Marty and your mom."

"If that is the case, then I should be able to hit the firewall hard."

"Great! Let's head to the conference room for our morning ritual."

Martinez stood and exited with Bobby on his heels.

After traveling all night, the jet carrying the two hostages landed at a private airport. They were then taken to a secure area and placed into separate cells. The flex-cuffs and masks were removed, and they were given a hot meal. Not a meal consistent with bread and water, as portrayed in the movies. This meal was exquisite, as if provided by a five-star restaurant sided with a decadent dessert. They looked at each other through the bars of their adjoining cells, perplexed by the meal given them by masked men in black combat uniforms; the contrast of elegance and brutality was ironic.

One hour later, after the morning brief, Bobby returned to his office and called Albright. Something he had never done before, but precedence overtook protocol. No answer. Bobby immediately dialed again. No answer. The urgency of protecting Albright and himself from DeLorean and his sister was the key item on the list of chores. He sat back in the chair, wondering if Albright had done anything and, if not, what he should do to ensure their cover remained intact. He hated waiting.

Albright ignored the two calls from Bobby. He was engaged in a conversation that trumped Bobby's OCD. After hanging up, he texted Bobby a message that acknowledged he saw the missed calls and provided some fatherly insight about his impatience. "And let patience have its full effect, that you may be perfect and complete, lacking in nothing."

Martinez knocked on the door and Bobby motioned him in. Bobby was holding his cell phone and focused on the screen. He shook his head and let puffed out a "humph" sound.

Martinez noticed an unusual gesture. "Are you ok?"

Bobby looked up. "Your grandfather is driving me crazy. I ask for information regarding our situation, and he responds with a Bible verse about my lack of patience. I cannot, we cannot afford to sit around wondering what his plans are…if he even has plans to contain this situation."

Martinez laughed. "If he is sending you Bible verses, everything is under control. You can relax."

Bobby stared at Martinez for a moment. "Are you sure?" Martinez nodded. "Ok. We will continue to review the surveillance reports as if nothing is wrong."

Martinez nodded again. "Nothing is wrong with my grandfather. However, Gold caught something on the radar after our meeting and shared it with me. That's why I'm standing here."

"What is it?"

"I think he needs to tell you."

Bobby began typing. "I'm sending out an email for our team to meet in the conference room in 10 minutes."

Martinez raised his eyebrows. "That was fast. I need to hit the head first. See you in a few."

The team was forever punctual and dedicated to the mission. After some informal salutations and a joke or two, Bobby called the meeting to order and thanked everyone for being on time. "Each of you knows I would not have called an impromptu meeting on such short notice unless it was regarding something important, and it seems Gold has struck gold. The members acknowledged Gold via half-hearted salutes, golf claps, and thumbs up, accompanied by laughter. Moments like this galvanized the team because unity was their collaborative core value. Even though they were not *Musketeers*, "*All for one and one for all*," was the perfect motto that defined their collective character.

Bobby enjoyed their light-hearted attitude and ravenous dedication to completing each objective successfully. "Let's get the show on the road. Gold, before you share your discovery, please enlighten us about the source."

> *"Was it CIA, NSA, Interpol, FBI, or MI6?"*

Gold smiled. "None of the above. Neither foreign nor domestic. I stumbled upon it while reading various news sources on the Internet last night."

Everyone's face reflected surprise. Bobby inquired. "How can you trust a source from a news agency that is fueled by sensationalism and the bottom line?"

Gold kept smiling. "I knew you would ask that question. This morning, I contacted our sources in NSA and CIA. It seems they were surprised to know the information had been published before they shared it with the Commander-in-Chief. The information is valid."

Bobby shook his head. "I need to contact them."

Martinez interrupted. "No can do, sir! Remember, as a colonel for Spain, you have access to almost every source of information and intelligence agency, but there are some restrictions. This is one of those restrictions. Information that hasn't been cleared and classified, even though it is on the Internet, cannot be shared with you via any domestic intelligence agency. That's why I asked Gold to contact the CIA and NSA for us before I spoke with you."

Bobby frowned. "That never happened to Major Brooks." Everyone looked at each other stoically. Then Bobby laughed. They joined in. "Martinez and Gold, great job! Just like each of us. Gold the floor is yours."

"Thanks, sir. This will take a few minutes, but I know everybody will notice once I share the information. China has previously and repeatedly denied any association regarding unauthorized access, 'hacking', into businesses or governments in other countries. Well, guess what?" Everyone laughed. "You already know the answer...they lied to us."

A collective "duh!" resonated in the room.

Gold smiled and continued. "Intelligence is showing Chinese hackers are getting more sophisticated. This evolution of ferreting into secure networks shows they are improving with continued impunity. Even though we know that China-supported criminals have infiltrated many networks, they continue to deny involvement as more attacks on various governments and business networks are perpetrated. We know China-nexus hacking groups are responsible because their modus operandi is to hack systems that are not typical targets of cyber espionage. They gain access by using techniques designed to evade common cybersecurity tools and detection."

Bobby interrupted. "Were the breaches discovered by the CIA or NSA?"

Gold shook his head. "No. The culprits were discovered by researchers at Google's Mandiant division."

"That is an interesting twist to our fight against network security breaches."

Martinez chimed in. "It looks like big business is becoming more and more involved in fighting cybercrime. This should help stop it."

Bobby shook his head. "No way!"

Everyone looked perplexed. "Why not? Isn't that our objective...success?"

Bobby stood and began pacing the room. "Do you really think we want to stop cybercrime?"

Everyone exchanged glances. "Yes!"

Bobby grinned. "Not in a million years. In fact, never. I'm going to share something with you that will make each of you question your position and responsibilities."

The room was silent.

"The economy of America is not sustainable by success. It is sustainable by failure."

Gold raised his hand. "Why would you even say that? All we hear and see is that our efforts are to win at everything we do. Americans are supposed to be the icon of success."

"That's what we are led to believe. Lies! However, if we are successful at everything we do, we would put ourselves out of business. Therefore, ironically, for us to succeed, we must fail. Let me share a few examples with you. Our economy does not rely on food, oil, gas, or natural resources. It relies on war. War, war, war is a mantra to get Americans involved."

Martinez interrupted. "We are not at war now. That fact dispels your theory."

"Ostensibly, yes. That is what we are conditioned to believe. Let's consider some events of the past 100 years. What took us out of the *Great Depression*?"

Again, everyone exchanged glances until Gold answered questionably. "*World War II*?"

Bobby smiled. "Yes. What did we do five years after World War II? We entered the *Korean Conflict*. Then, less than ten years later, we entered *the Vietnam War*. It wasn't until the *Vietnam War people began* to see the results of war."

Bobby looked at their expressions. "Broken hearts, broken homes, and broken promises replaced, 'For God and Country,' as Americans revolted against our involvement in Vietnam. Was this the beginning to end wars?" Bobby smiled. "Yes, and no. It was time to step away from conventional wars because people were overwhelmed with the prices we paid. We had to save ourselves. Our politicians didn't miss a beat. They created domestic wars to keep taxpayer dollars rolling in while supporting big business, their investments, their lobbyists, and their political agendas. Their fake wars heralded help for the people. We needed to change negatives into positives. So, they created battles to fight negative things in America. We created the war on poverty, free food, free housing, and free medical services to help our impoverished citizens. We created the war on illiteracy to help people improve intellectually by providing materials, books, and services. Ironically, we spend more money on educating students than any other nation, yet lag far behind the rest of the world intellectually. Not a good return on investment, so we continued to invest more money in a failed program."

Some of the team members laughed. Gold spoke. "That sounds about right. Let's put more money and effort into something that will never change. Isn't that the definition of insanity?"

Bobby smiled. "Exactly the point! However, you will discover these domestic wars improved nothing. Now, to the king of domestic spending, the war that siphons more tax dollars every year than any other. The war on drugs. This was the war that brought battles onto the streets of our cities. We were going to fight the drug dealers and cartels using military weapons, tactics, and combat mentality. Police were immediately transformed into Soldiers expected to kill anyone perceived as a threat.

This created an actual battlefield at home. However, if we stopped drug production and marketing, it would lead to a reduction of law enforcement jobs, prisons, rehabilitation, and other associated services."

> *We could stop drugs from entering America, but we won't.*

The war on drugs was better than expected. So, we took the battles to new heights. We broadened the war on crime by building more prisons – the prison industrial complex, more rehabilitation, and more tax dollars to fund the hiring of more police officers, guards, counselors, and structures. We are currently entrenched in the war on terrorism; we use war to bring fear, then we use fear to bring reliance, and in the end, we use reliance to bring servitude. We don't want solutions we want a continuation of every war. The medical forum is the same. They don't want cures for diseases and viruses, they want money for research and cures that never come. They put you on a drug regimen for the rest of your life to help you maintain your quality of life when in reality it pays for new cars, houses, and huge bank accounts that improve their quality of life. Imagine if a cure for cancer was produced, which has probably happened, everything in the medical-industrial complex related to cancer research and treatment would collapse. Think about this, there hasn't been a successful vaccination since polio. We don't want to stop illegal drugs. That would lead to the termination of police agencies, counselors, rehabilitation centers, and body bags. I know this sounds dark, but it is the truth. Our purpose is not to stop anything, but to show that we are trying. We present false hope to the public as they keep investing. The masses become the prisoners of those who gain the most from these created wars…the politicians, corporations, and investors."

"Nobody goes to Washington DC a millionaire but they all leave as one."

"The comprehension that America's motives were planned to give a false perception of good when in reality it is nothing more than a money-making scheme used by every administration regardless of political affiliation. They are all in bed with each other. The two parties exist to divide America while united in financial gain and opportunity. The room was silent. Bobby stood looking at the faces of each member. Their expressions were identical…blank.

Bobby cleared his throat as if to snap them out of a trance. "I realize I said too much, but we must know our mission and the truth of it."

Gold spoke. "Sir, that was incredible, and it makes perfect sense. How did you come up with these perspectives?"

"I didn't come up with anything. For the past several months I have been exposed to a series of documents that have records, first-hand accounts, of the Executive and Congressional branches of our government involved in crimes against humanity, graft, espionage, and murder. These documents contain facts so critical that people are willing to kill and be killed to get them."

Gold's mouth went agape. "That's why you got the identity change. You are a target."

Everyone looked back and forth at Bobby and the other team members. This moment was never expected and it would never be forgotten.

Martinez asked. "If this is so secretive why have you told us?"

"Because wherever I am they might show up and if I am here you better keep those weapons at the ready."

Everything was coming together. The change of identity, the surveillance of Europe, the attempted hacks, and the closing of the sixth floor.

Martinez continued. "So, the people who once inhabited the sixth floor, were they part of this conspiracy?"

Bobby pursed his lips. "Yes. Each was a top-secret operative in the world of espionage. It was determined after the *Manhattan Project*, any critical asset was to be managed to avoid the release of protected information that could embarrass or compromise the United States or an administration. After years of monitoring these retired operators, it was decided to bring them to an area where nobody knew them and manage them without costly operations. To save a nickel they were sentenced to die in obscurity. That was their retirement reward for their dedication."

"Did their families just hand them over to the government to disappear?"

"Never! They were kidnapped or killed in the presence of witnesses to cover the tracks of illegal government imprisonment and murder. Their families would die without knowing what happened to half of them."

"Are you a critical asset?"

"Yes. An attempt to assassinate me a few weeks ago proves that somebody wants me dead. Therefore, I shared this with you. It's obvious they know who I am and where I am. I don't trust them. They can come here and expect zero resistance. However, we are ready."

"Sir, do you think they can get into the facility?"

Bobby stared. "I believe they have inside help from someone high in this administration. If that is the case, they will have the passcodes. We cannot afford to let our guard down. Are each of you ready if they arrive?"

"Sir, each of us is a combat-experienced operator. We are always ready. Thank you for sharing this with us. I will speak to the team. We are with you and will do whatever is necessary to protect you and our mission."

Bobby lowered his head. "Thank you. I expected nothing less. I've told you more than I should have, but I could never live with myself if anything happened to you because I kept a secret. Let's get back to work."

"Sir, will you give us permission to get extra magazines from the armory?"

"Get whatever you want. From this moment forward, you will take your weapons and ammo with you. Be on the alert." Each went to the armory and returned to their office with more resources. They were ready.

TAKEN - Chapter 25

DeLorean and Kuka took detailed notes of Marty's movements from when she arrived at the *Smithsonian* to when she left. This was the opportunity DeLorean had waited for…to follow her to her haven. After trailing her for about 20 minutes, she arrived at a posh motel with a gated parking garage. She used her room key to open the electric gates and park her vehicle. Once she entered the garage, DeLorean lost visual contact with her. He pulled up to the front door as if checking in and walked to the front desk. He asked questions regarding the establishment and the amenities. He told the receptionist he was considering staying here when he returned with his family while on vacation. The receptionist was very accommodating and provided excellent information. DeLorean complemented the young female on her impeccable expertise and asked if he could look around. She told him to check out the dining area, the pool, the gym, and the lounge. He nodded his head and, after walking out of sight, quickly entered the stairwell and scanned each floor, hoping to see where Marty lived. Nothing. As he was turning to the 5th-floor stairwell door, he glanced over his shoulder to see Marty walking with the ice bucket in hand. She was focused on the door and not spilling the ice.

She placed the card key over the sensor, the door unlocked, and she entered.

After hearing the door securely, he stealthily walked down the hall and made a mental note of the room number. He quickly exited the establishment. As soon as he closed the car door, Kuka was asking questions. "Did you find her?"

After securing his seat belt, he turned toward her and smiled. She knew the answer was "yes".

DeLorean nodded in approval. "We have everything we need to begin our surveillance tomorrow."

Kuka smiled. "Finally! We are back on track to find Albright."

They nodded in unison. DeLorean took the afternoon off to ensure he had time to review the potential scenarios with Kuka. As they drove, they outlined various options and detailed how they would observe the target. Their endeavor would begin at 0700 near the *Smithsonian*. Kuka slept well for the first time after many sleepless nights.

Marty was oblivious that she had been followed. The only thing occupying her thoughts was that Bobby was no longer in the building and should anything happen, she would have to call him. She felt vulnerable. After showering and eating a light dinner, she settled in with some of Albright's notes in hand. She began the review and documentation process that would be shared later with Bobby. Two hours later, she placed the documents and her review on the table and then retired for the evening.

Less than ten minutes away, Bobby and Martinez sat in the living room suite at the new location. They began by reviewing several areas of concern regarding the operations and information provided by the team. One hour later, they concluded the official business and took to the covert operation. Bobby began the conversation about DeLorean and his sister. He detailed the activities he expected DeLorean to orchestrate. He knew DeLorean would arrive early and station themselves at two locations, preferably high ground, that would allow them to have an unobstructed view of Dr. Martinez and Marty's outdoor activities.

Martinez asked, "Will we be there watching them?"

Bobby nodded. "Yes, we will shadow them from a location they would not expect."

Martinez nodded in agreement. "Where will we be located?"

Bobby smiled. "I don't know." He laughed.

Martinez. "Do you think that is an appropriate answer?"

"Yes, because I do not know where I will station myself. Regardless, we need to have the upper hand. That's why we need to arrive earlier than them. With that, let me give you the communications equipment you will use while observing human commerce at the Finnish Embassy."

Martinez raised his eyebrows. "The Finnish Embassy! Why there?"

Bobby reached into a black bag that was on the floor next to the couch. He removed a box that contained the military-issued, long-range communications system that hid perfectly on the body and handed it to Martinez. "Remember, his sister works from there. I'm hoping she will stop by before she settles in to monitor your mom and Marty."

Martinez secured the box. "Roger that! What about my clothing?"

Bobby laughed, then went blank. "Make it simple, comfortable, and able to hide your pistol and two extra magazines."

Martinez read Bobby's facial expression perfectly. "Yes, sir. Do I bring and secure my M4 in the car?"

"No. That would be nice, but we cannot risk the possibility of your car being compromised or stolen. Ironically, the icon of capitalism has one of the highest crime rates in America. I have already set the frequency on the radios. We will be on a scrambled, secure frequency. I will make the radio check at 0645. Be ready."

"Sounds great. I will be onsite by that time. What is the protocol if I observe her in my AO?"

"Contact me. After we determine her direction of travel, we will make the tactical decision at that time." Bobby stood. Martinez mirrored. They shook hands. "Get some rest, sergeant. Tomorrow can be very boring or high-speed."

"I hear that." They walked to the door and Martinez left.

Bobby looked at his watch. It was time for a shower and bed. He hoped tomorrow would be exciting, but high-profile observations were usually ninety-nine percent sitting and one percent insanity. He slept well.

The Aristocrat was pleased with the post-operation report he received regarding the first phase, securing two soft targets. The next phase would share similar operational steps and procedures that would produce a similar result. Stealthily moving a team in and out of crowds while observing and ultimately kidnapping people required detailed observations of the target's daily activities for not less than two weeks. These observations lead to the discovery of target habits that provided the perfect time and location to engage. Once this phase was complete, the next two phases would be highly complicated. He would meet with the Commander and review the details to ensure everything was outlined perfectly. He would accept nothing but success.

AWAKENING - Chapter 26

It was as if Brooks, DeLorean, Martinez, and Kuka were connected at the brain stem because they shared similar operating characteristics, mission objectives, and situational awareness. Their actions would emulate the meeting of two chess masters methodically assessing each other's moves before moving. This was the meeting of the minds between DeLorean and Bobby, and only one would win. Let the pieces fall as they may! Each departed to their predesignated destination. Four people independent in objectives but collaborative in mentality. As Bobby predicted, DeLorean and Kuka took the high ground, Martinez was watching the Finnish Embassy, and Bobby sat disheveled in a wheelchair outside the Smithsonian as a homeless veteran. Each professional was transfixed on locating Marty or Dr. Martinez in the crowds. Almost on cue, they all spotted Marty walking toward the *Smithsonian,* with Dr. Martinez a few steps behind her. In less than a minute, they entered the complex. Bobby knew Marty would not depart for lunch until 11:30. She loved to beat the crowds. He contacted Martinez to meet at the predesignated rally point. They returned to the office. The waiting game began.

Albright spent the night in his office. Marty and Dr. Martinez were surprised to discover him cooking eggs, hash browns, and ham in the kitchenette. The smell of fresh coffee added to the atmosphere of home cooking; it was heavenly to Marty, who had been trying a fashion diet for a month. The ladies joined Albright in the kitchenette a few minutes after arriving. They chit-chatted about the smell of the breakfast and how the coffee was so delicious. Albright asked Marty how the document review was progressing. She assured him it was proceeding fine and that her outlines were succinctly aligned with the original content. Albright told the ladies he was engaged in some research and fell asleep at his desk. They laughed. They visited for about 20 minutes before returning to their offices. Before they walked out of the kitchenette, Albright asked the ladies what time they were going to lunch. Dr. Martinez said, "Are you suggesting we get out of the office for lunch? If so, are you buying?" They laughed as Albright responded. "Yes. I will buy it if we leave at 11:30. I hate crowds." They looked at each other and nodded. Lunch would begin at 11:30.

After reviewing the field reports and submitting the results to his supervisor, William Martin sat at his desk and began sipping an energy drink. The early afternoon attacks from *Sand Man* made his eyes droop and see double vision. The walk to the vending machine helped kick-start the process of awakening. His phone rang and the caller ID showed "Unknown." Normally, he would have forwarded the call to voice mail, but he knew speaking with someone, even a telemarketer, to help him wake up.

He answered generically.

The caller responded by asking if William Martin was available. This was unexpected and immediately raised his suspicions because this was a secure line and if it was a computerized autodial, the caller would not know his name. His mind kicked in and erased any sleep issues. "May I ask who is calling, please?"

"Of course. I am Colonel Roberto Arrollos from Spain trying to contact William Martin."

This was an unexpected call. "Colonel, what a wonderful surprise." Martin tried to embellish the call with positiveness.

"I appreciate your time. I hope I'm not interrupting anything."

"No, sir. I am available. How may I assist you?"

"Great. I'm reaching out to see if your field operators have noticed the recent activity from China or Germany?"

The past 30 seconds were full of surprises. "Nothing has passed my desk. Why do you ask?"

"While my field operators have attempted to infiltrate several Chinese Internet trunks and breach their networks, an unexpected source has revealed some interesting information. Their research has provided us Full Monty."

William laughed. "Full Monty? That's something I never expected to hear in the espionage business. Am I to understand you mean you can see everything clearly?"

The answer was accompanied by laughter. "Yes sir. It seems the Chinese have developed some powerful hacking resources and our professionals at Google caught them in the act. Our unfriendly adversaries are connected to a suspected China-nexus hacking group. Their MO is to target software on computers that don't have antivirus or endpoint detection software."

"Why would that be of consequence with us? Unprotected systems are usually personal and are limited to home networks."

"Exactly! We, however, initially discovered some unprotected home systems used by military and government personnel, who have disregarded the protocols dictated by the government and military, have opened gateways into secure networks if the login history is properly backtracked."

Martin spoke slowly as he tapped his index finger on his chin. "That proposes a problem."

"There is more! During the research, it was also discovered that the targets also include corporate systems designed to protect companies. Their talents are evolving and so do the threats. Now the worst news."

Martin interrupted. "It gets worse?"

"Unfortunately, it does. We cannot monitor every attempt to hack our systems. The Chinese are promoting thousands of intrusion activities each day and a majority go undetected. The experts at *Google* told us the problem is bigger than we know and growing daily."

"I'm sitting here shocked, but not shocked if you know what I mean. We all suspect these activities are happening, but never want to accept threats they possess."

"I share your thoughts. Do you have anything you can share with me?"

Martin shook his head. "No. Nothing of consequence after what you just told me."

"We will stay in contact. I appreciate everything. Oh, I want to thank you for giving me access to the network. It is a valuable resource for all of us. Do you mind if I send you the report on China's growing threats?"

"Not at all. I appreciate it."

"It is sent. Let me know when you receive it."

"Got it. Thanks again."

"Thank you."

Bobby ended the call and looked at Martinez. "Did you get it?"

"Yes, sir. Without a heads-up, I could never have traced the IP address to their servers. This will help me get access to their network."

Bobby smiled. "Awesome. Now all you need to do is get past the firewall."

"We have resources for that. I'll keep you posted."

"Thank you. Hey, before you leave, remember we have a lunch date at 11:00." Martinez smiled and left, the laptop in hand with the screen still open. He was focused. "I'll be here."

Marty looked at her watch, hoping it was 11:30. She was disappointed, realizing she would have to wait another 30 minutes before leaving for lunch. Hitting the snooze button too many times seemed appropriate. Now, later in the morning, she was starving because she didn't have enough time to eat breakfast. The kitchenette was void of food, so she would have to wait. She heard someone say, "Hey."

She turned around to see Albright standing in the doorway. "What are you doing at this neck of the woods?"

Albright smiled. "Looking for you. I have a proposition for you."

Marty's eyes widened. "Really? What's up, doc?" She laughed. "I didn't realize I just quoted the famous animated philosopher *Bugs Bunny*."

Albright laughed. "It's not like I haven't heard that before. Anyway. I need the office and you need a break. How about you take off for at least a couple of hours? I'll call you when I finish, then you can return. Are you ok with that?"

Marty's eyes stayed wide with delight. "Sure! When can I leave?"

Albright grinned. "Now."

"I'm outta here! See you around one." Marty picked up her purse and was gone in an instant.

Albright took out his cell phone and pressed the shortcut button for a common number in the address book. "Hello."

Albright spoke. "The rabbit has left the hole. Are there foxes in the field?"

"Yes. Two foxes and the hunter are watching them."

"Tell the hunter to stand by. See you in a few."

"Yes, sir." Albright hung up and placed the phone in his pocket. After returning to his office, he put his earbuds on, then sunglasses, and walked out of the building.

DeLorean had been eyeballing the exits all morning when he saw an elderly man wearing sunglasses leave through the doors used by Marty and Dr. Martinez. He reached for his radio and before he could push the transmit button, Kuka was already checking to see if he had made a visual of the likely target.

"Yes, I see him."

"Is that Albright?"

"I need to get a better look." He began walking toward the entrance so he would pass close to the man and verify his suspicions. As he got closer, the man stopped and extended his hand. "Major DeLorean. How are you today?"

DeLorean immediately stopped and began scanning the area. Kuka was on the radio asking why he stopped. Albright walked to him and stopped directly in his path. "Why didn't you shake my hand? You have been looking for me and here I am."

DeLorean knew he had been played and shook his head. "You think you are so smart, doctor, but I'm letting you know we are watching you."

Albright smiled. "We. Are you saying your sister and you? If that's the case let's get together over a cup of java." DeLorean looked behind himself and saw Kuka walking in between two men who would have played pro football without the pads. Albright smiled. "Please follow me or I will be forced to throw you away with the trash. Albright held his hand next to DeLorean's face. On the palm was a small red dot that slowly moved in DeLorean's direction.

Albright stared at his forehead.

"That dot in the middle of your forehead is where the bullet will enter if I give the signal. You don't mean anything to me, but I need to ask you a few questions. By the way, if you think I'm angry because you put me in that dungeon to die…you are correct. Again, don't give me the satisfaction of spraying your gray matter all over the sidewalk." The escorts arrived with Kuka. Albright looked at her and grinned. "So, you are the black widow. So nice to meet you. How about you follow me to my web? Let's go." Everyone followed Albright to the entrance. He used his CAC to gain entry and a few minutes later DeLorean and Kuka were handcuffed to a pair of heavy cast-iron chairs in the vault. Before saying anything, Albright made a call on his cell phone. "Hello, remember I told you I might need more time? Yes. Take the afternoon off. I'll see you in the morning."

Albright dismissed the goons and began speaking with DeLorean and Kuka in private.

Bobby and Martinez arrived. They tactically positioned themselves to watch in four directions, hoping to see DeLorean and Kuka. After 30 minutes, nothing. After 90 minutes, nothing. They continued this protocol until 5:00 pm. Still no sign of DeLorean and Kuka. Bobby made the call to stay until 6:00 pm to see if DeLorean and Kuka would show up. Then, immediately after talking to Martinez, he saw Dr. Albright exit the building. Bobby hid in the shadows, out of the flow of pedestrians and tourists. Albright was walking oblivious of Bobby when he pivoted and walked directly to him. "Tell Martinez to meet us here. We have a meeting to attend, and I don't want to wait." Seconds later, Martinez arrived.

Albright looked at them. "Rookies! I had you spotted like you were wearing signs that said, 'Hey mom, look at me. I'm hiding from Dr. Albright.'" Bobby and Martinez looked at each other, thinking the same thing about Albright.

"Listen carefully. I will meet you at 8:00 pm." He pulled out two business cards and handed one to each man. "This is the location. Don't be late. Is that understood?" Both men nodded in agreement. "Now get out of here before anyone spots us." Bobby and Martinez were unaware that Albright had DeLorean and Kuka secured in the tomb of artifacts area. Ten minutes later, Albright was at the front gate getting security checked before entering the apartment complex. He took no chances. Bobby and Martinez shared thoughts, wondering how an elderly man could outwit them and make them surrender to his demands. Everyone was tired.

They sat in the cells. Everything was silent, unless the guards changed duty stations or walked around the perimeter to perform welfare checks. They sat in the cells. Everything was silent, unless the guards changed duty stations, delivered a five-star meal, or walked the perimeter to perform welfare checks. The only access to freedom was a small window that had a sliding cover reminiscent of a speak-easy and a slot where the food was delivered. There was no contact with others or daylight, it was a depressing situation. Fortunately, the bed and bedding provided comfort and warmth; something not provided in a prison. Whatever the situation, the waiting game was as enjoyable as Chinese water torture. Less than twelve inches away, on the other side of a shared wall, these same thoughts were entertained by the other kidnapped victim.

The Aristocrat was eager to complete the mission. There were a couple of loose ends that needed to be completed before the initial phases of the operation were complete and the next steps would begin. The desk phone rang. He answered it. The conversation was a staccato of 'yes' and 'no' responses to the other person's questions. He hung up the phone. His signature evil grin graced his face. He loved his office. He loved opulence. He loved himself. But more than anything, he loved his power and the thought of being known throughout the world as a leader who was to be feared. Life was good, and it would soon become great.

Marty was enjoying the relaxation of an afternoon of freedom. This was unusual, and she was going to get the most out of it. During this gleeful moment, she failed to notice she was being followed by an SUV with two male occupants.

QUESTIONS - Chapter 27

Albright returned and began asking DeLorean and Kuka a series of questions. The goons sat DeLorean and Kuka less than a foot apart side-by-side facing Albright, who had turned the chair around and used the backrest to support his arms. "Well, fancy meeting you here." Albright laughed. "I guess you both were surprised to see me. Now that we are together, you can relax. I don't plan on killing either of you, but if the opportunity arises, I'm sure I will be quick and painless." They stared at Albright with contempt, but said nothing. "Kuka, if I may, because I hate calling you the Black Widow, it sounds so sinister, and you seem like such a wonderful church lady. Are Finland's President, Embassy, and Prime Minister's Office know you are a contractor for the United States government?" Kuka could not hide the surprise on her face when Albright spoke about her covert operations with the United States. She said nothing, but her expression was telling.

Albright smiled. "Your silence is exactly what I expected. Spies stay silent when captured. They don't say anything. They are expected to take a trip down the cyanide capsule and escape. Then their lifeless body falls to the floor as froth drips from their mouth like a rabid dog." He expressed a sarcastic smile and flex of his eyebrows. "Of course, the movies make it seem so heroic, yet grotesque. Anyway, let me dispense with the Hollywood novelties and chatter. I wonder what would happen if I made a call to one of my Finnish dignitaries and shared the information regarding your mercenary duties with other nations. I believe that would question your allegiance to Finland and possibly remove you from your nice cushy office for prison."

DeLorean was frustrated. "What do you want, Albright? I'm a member of the United States military who has been detained without due process — kidnapped!"

Albright looked at DeLorean and grinned, nodding and pointing a right index finger at him. "Yes. Yes, you are a member of the United States military who has not been kidnapped. You are part of an impromptu meeting with a member of another United States entity seeking specific answers to covert domestic operations, which, by the way, are highly suspect and questionable."

The expression of frustration waned from DeLorean's face. "If this is, as you say, a legitimate impromptu meeting, then why am I handcuffed? Also, why is a member from the Finnish Embassy here if this is a domestic matter? Or has it evolved to a quorum?"

"That's an impressive notation to our shindig. How about we say this is an investigation of treasonous activities regarding your participation, acting under the authority of a rogue political entity, who targeted and/or murdered former United States counter-operations personnel? Everyone you detained illegally was a citizen and denied the same due process you are whining about. Does that make you feel better?"

DeLorean had never met Albright before, but their first encounter was leaving a bad taste in his mouth. "You have no authority to detain me for questioning. I demand my immediate release."

"I wouldn't have expected anything less, and I have an answer to your demands. I am still a counter-intelligence operative...surprise! Which means I have the authority to detain and question you until I believe you have complied. Don't you just love the *Patriot Act*?"

DeLorean blurted out. "Are you suggesting you can hold us indefinitely?"

Albright stood and began pacing. "No, I would never suggest I could hold you indefinitely. However, in this case, I can and will hold you indefinitely if necessary." DeLorean looked at Kuka. He knew his sister well. Her eyes spoke volumes, even though she remained silent and expressionless. "I refuse to answer. I cannot incriminate myself and am protected under the law."

"Under normal circumstances, that would be true. However, your activities regarding rogue operations within the military and government are treasonous, which forces me to find answers to and use whatever tools necessary to encourage your participation and cooperation."

DeLorean stiffened in the seat. "Are you suggesting torture?"

"Here we go again. Semantics. I'm not suggesting anything, I'm stating a fact. After our last encounter, I will gladly use whatever means possible to get the answers. Do you understand? Remember what you did to me?"

Kuka wasn't included in the conversation, but she knew Albright was serious about incorporating creative methods of motivation. For an older man, Albright seemed to have the zeal of a war criminal. Who knows, maybe he is a war criminal.

Albright stopped pacing. "Well, beloved. I have another meeting to attend and must be leaving. My two friends will make sure you are comfortable as you answer their questions. If not, they will show you their specialized skills of inciting conversation. I would do as instructed. Answer their questions. This will help you avoid some mental, emotional, and physical scars." Albright nodded as he turned to leave. The goons arose and walked toward them. Kuka and DeLorean exchanged glances. They knew there was only one option. Albright disappeared.

PART FOUR

ENLIGHTENMENT

REVELATION - Chapter 28

Bobby and Martinez arrived a few minutes early at the location noted on the business card. They were in a large vacant parking lot surrounded by various-sized buildings. It resembled an old industrial park.

Bobby did a visual perimeter scan using his night vision goggles. He took no chances. Martinez felt the *Sig Sauer P220* underneath his untucked shirt. Bobby was carrying an identical pistol. They continued scanning until headlights showed a vehicle was approaching. Bobby left the car engine running in case they needed to distance themselves from a threat. The headlights on the vehicle turned off as it closed the distance and pulled next to the driver. Bobby and Martinez secured their pistols. The tinted window on the driver's side of the vehicle slowly lowered, revealing the smiling face of Dr. Albright. "Good evening, gentlemen. Fancy meeting you here."

Bobby shook his head. "Where is here?" Martinez shrugged his shoulders in the background.

"This is my hidden office location. Follow me." Bobby and Martinez exchanged glances, knowing Albright had sprung another surprise on them. As Albright slowly drove away, Bobby turned the car around and followed. They stopped in front of a three-story building resembling something from a 1940s movie.

The antiquated door had a contemporary keypad above the handle. Albright entered a series of numbers, then pressed 'Enter.' The sound of a mechanical mechanism lasted for about five seconds. The door unlocked. Albright pulled the handle, and the perfectly balanced 900-pound armor-resistance door moved effortlessly.

Bobby did not expect a fortified door. "What's with the Fort Knox security?"

Albright smiled and winked. "Follow me and you will see!" He stepped inside with Bobby and Martinez following. The door closed automatically. As they walked, motion sensors activated lights along the sterile hall. Ironically, there were no nameplates on the doors, reminiscent of the 6th floor.

As they walked, Albright continued the tour. "This is my weekend getaway, as I call it! The building has a cooling and heating system on the outer walls to trick any infrared searches, trying to see if there is internal activity. The windows are fake, highly detailed images, impervious to the elements, that overlay the metal skin of the outside walls. Directly below us is an array of supercomputers hidden in the vault, accessed by two people. This is my playland, the place where my dreams come true." Bobby quietly told himself. "Playland? Albright sounded more like *Willy Wonka* than one of the smartest people in the world. He was obsessed with this facility, which was understandable because of its vast resources."

Albright stopped at door seven. He placed his right hand on the touchpad and the door opened. He motioned for Bobby and Martinez to follow. Albright spoke, "Lights." And the room revealed itself. Bobby quickly realized why Albright was obsessed. The room resembled the best science fiction operations center ever imagined. The computers came to life, revealing several large monitors on the four walls that displayed various satellite views of the world with location information automatically scrolling. Two of the walls accommodated four workstations, each had three 36-inch monitors and noise-canceling headsets. The chairs were ergonomic, with gel inserts and adjustable settings that went beyond the common high backs found in most offices. The centerpiece of the room was a large black lacquered conference table with twelve chairs on each side and one chair at each end. In the middle of the table was a white, silver, and black accented logo etched into the wood that displayed the Greek word "SKOTOS." The directional overhead lighting was adjusted to place focus on the table and logo, which darkened the surrounding workstations and walls. Secondary lighting was provided by the large wall monitors that cast a spectrum of colors throughout the room as the screen images changed. Martinez was beside himself. "What the heck is this? Are we on board the *Star Trek Enterprise* or on a *Star Wars* movie set? This is incredible."

Albright looked at each man. "This, gentlemen, is the location, my brainchild, of global operations. This state-of-the-art facility is second to none. Welcome to SKOTOS. You are ordered never to say anything about this facility or its location. This is beyond classified. There are only five other people on the planet that know of its existence, and one of them will arrive shortly."

Bobby scanned the room. He, like Martinez, was mesmerized by the enormity of technology and atmosphere. "I imagined no one, especially you, Dr. Albright, would have something of this magnitude. It exceeds NORAD. How is it possible to operate a facility of this size with no personnel on-site?"

"My operators work remotely. If we meet in this location, it is because of a situation requiring utmost attention and urgency."

Bobby made eye contact with Albright. "Am I to presume we are here because of an urgent situation?"

Albright nodded. "Yes. In a few minutes, you and Martinez will be privy to some of the most classified secret information regarding the United States for the past seven decades. You will also be briefed about your promotions and the associated responsibilities required to work in our operations branch."

Martinez stepped out of the professional character bubble. "Grandpa! New position in operations? Why haven't you ever told me about this place?"

"Until today, you have never had the maturity or experience to become a member of this elite team. Today you graduate into the big leagues." Albright patted him on the back.

The moment was interrupted as a buzzer broke the silence as a smaller security monitor showed someone at the entrance. An instant later, the word "AUTHORIZED" appeared on the screen and the person entered the facility.

A moment later, a man in a navy-blue polo shirt and khaki pants entered.

His brown hair with gray accents projected an air of aristocracy. Albright met him with a handshake and walked him toward Bobby. "Gentlemen, I would like to introduce one of my most trusted confidants and operators. We will refer to him as Sheppard." Bobby extended his hand. "Nice to meet you, Sheppard." Martinez stepped up and did the same. Albright walked to the head seat at the table and motioned for the men to sit. "Before we continue, Sheppard is aware of your official title, Colonel Arrollos." Bobby nodded. "Sheppard currently wears two hats. He is our direct contact and has an office at MI6 headquarters. Second, he is our attaché assigned to the British Army Special Air Service (SAS)."

Sheppard unexpectedly exclaimed, "*Who Dares Wins!*"

Bobby laughed as he recognized the SAS motto. "*Who Dares Wins!* I worked those guys when I was downrange in the sandbox."

Sheppard gave a thumbs up with a nod of his head.

Albright snapped his fingers. Everyone looked at him. "Time is wasting. Now, to the purpose of us being here. We are here to review the elements in my dossier and create a plan to execute operations to fight against those wanting to destroy America and me. Please sit down."

Albright looked at Sheppard. "I'm sorry I didn't ask earlier. How was your trip?"

"No problem. Fortunately, it was uneventful but long. However, I had time to review your information and support your decision to bring these two men on board as operators. We need additional and more experienced personnel."

Albright nodded, then opened the folder he had placed before him earlier. He touched the tabletop with his finger and dragged the tip across the mirrored surface. The mouse pointer on the main wall monitor reacted accordingly. Each man directed their attention to the monitor as Albright presented images and voiced information related to each. "Several decades ago, I became a member, actually a unique person, attached to the Office of the President, who was FDR."

I shared in the details of presidential meetings with several historical dignitaries, beginning with Churchill. He identified pre- and post-war events that led to the creation and evolution of the atomic bomb and the beginning of the *Cold War*. He shared his anger about U.S. involvement in Korea and the quick decision to send American military personnel into South Vietnam.

Bobby raised his hand. "Dr. Albright, are you saying we joined Korea and South Vietnam as an avenue to maintain a stable economy while creating and supporting the creation of the *Military Industrial Complex*?"

"Amen! You have seen the light! Our presence in these battlegrounds differed from those of former wars. Our stance was to provide support from America with the tools of war, which included the loss of brave men and women. Tools require money and money makes people rich. The cycle of finances from military involvement had begun and, as you stated, strengthening the overarching power of the *Military Industrial Complex*. Before long, we sent smaller military units, tentacles, around the world as advisers and trainers. Then, if something went bad, we were already onsite and had a sense of what was happening. Albright went further by detailing what contributed to the paradigm shift regarding American involvement in wars. He noted that during the *Vietnam War*, an awakening began at home as young men and women pushed back and demanded we pull out from Southeast Asia. After the killing of four anti-war college students at *Kent State University* in Ohio, the President met increased hostilities from parents and students with additional support from veterans. The decision to withdraw was set into motion."

Albright stood. "Does anyone need to take a break?"

Bobby chimed in, "Yes. With all the technology here, where is the most fundamental room?"

Albright laughed. "Follow me everyone." He led them out of the room, took a right, and walked to the end of the hall, then pushed the door open. "Here you go! Everything is state-of-the-art. We have bidets, automatic water and soap dispensers, and ultraviolet light to ensure you kill all bacteria on your hands and body. This is a sterile environment."

Martinez laughed. "Sterile environment? This is beyond sterile. You could perform surgery on someone." Everyone laughed.

Albright smiled. "After you complete your business, return to the conference room, but press the door immediately across the hall and enter the dining and kitchen area. I will introduce you to the appliances and resources at your disposal and keep you alive if necessary." Twenty minutes later, they returned to the conference room with beverages and snacks.

After returning, Albright continued the briefing. "This unexpected pushback from people who hated the mindset of sending our youth to fight and die in other countries was the last straw for Americans to trust politicians. War was the key contributor to our economy. It pulled us out of the *Great Depression* and established a unified nation of patriots who valued freedom by fighting oppression. War was the word engrained in every American's mind that called us to collectively respond to aggressively defeat evil. This, however, began the evolution of the *Military Industrial Complex*. Large corporations and political influencers became wealthy elitists who took advantage of war and placed their investments in manufacturing, marketing, and distributing their products and materials around the world. Their influence over the political elite was obscene. Money and graft became the status quo of politicians as their lobbyists pushed for support and federal endorsements. This is when I realized no politician arrived in Washington as a millionaire, but everyone leaves as one. This mentality continues today as pseudo-wars have replaced conventional wars. The same mentality is applied, but instead of fighting outside of our borders, we fight within them."

Martinez interrupted. "Can you please elaborate on the pseudo-war topic?"

"Yes. The failures in Korea and Southeast Asia jaded Americans' belief that the United States was invincible. This realization produced a reverse motivation as people backed away from supporting war because of the high costs and losses. War was the cliché, the key to getting Americans to open their pocketbooks without question and fight the good fight. Unfortunately, this distrust and loss of faith in political leadership weakened the war machine. With big business pressure, investors persuaded politicians to create other threats that would unite taxpayers. So, we created pseudo-wars. Fake wars that gave the inside trader, politicians, and their friends insight into which areas of the government would need manpower and products. A corrupt method of marketing and making money, allowing investors security and the guarantee of huge windfalls from their investments. Their money, commerce, and enterprises were secretly identified, encouraged, and fueled by the greed of exclusive elitists and politicians whipping the backs of the taxpayer."

Martinez shook his head. "Why hasn't anyone said or done anything about that?"

Democrats and Republicans alike.

"We have tried! Unfortunately, lawyers create laws that guarantee themselves jobs, business opportunities, and above the law power. Lawyers are the majority in Washington, DC, as they promote their agendas. You and I can be arrested, tried, and sent to prison for life while politicians and their families routinely break laws, encourage graft, embrace insider trading, expect kickbacks, demand payoffs, and approve government contracts to their business cronies who line their pockets with millions of dollars."

Albright stood. "Republicans and Democrats are united in partaking of these crimes while ostensibly fighting with each other on behalf of one political party or the other. It's nothing more than a dog and pony show which continues its obscenity every day. When I discovered this, I was incensed and incorporated perspectives from other influential and trusted leaders worldwide who shared my viewpoints and supported the philosophy of fairness and peace, not the crimes brokered in Washington, DC. Unfortunately, the political machine continues to promote wars while pushing, bullying, leaders of weaker nations into corners behind the scenes and when these smaller nations came out swinging, we cried victims. It worked with the Japanese. They were pushed into an economic corner and fought instead of being bullied by FDR. We used the same aggression against Chile, Iran, Iraq, and several Middle Eastern countries until our plan worked better than imagined. Before long, our *Military Industrial Complex* was larger and more involved with the backing of our political and business criminals who sit in the Capital, the Whitehouse, in Fortune 500 businesses, on Wall Street, and in the arena of psychological operations rekindling aggression and war. The lottery arrived the moment Russia invaded Afghanistan. The world was incensed as news media reported biased perspectives, which made Russia the bully because they invaded a poor country with the sole purpose of defeating and overthrowing them. There were two things Russia did not expect: support from America using CIA operatives and Spec-Ops teams, and the rise of the Mujahideen, freedom fighters led by a little-known Yamani named Osama bin Laden. War, Jihad, was declared against Russia as thousands of Muslims from around the world joined forces to fight Russia. For ten years we provided weapons, military training, and reconnaissance while the Mujahideen sacrificed thousands of lives battling Russia."

Eventually, the support paid off and Russia withdrew.

"A success story about a defeated Russia graced headlines throughout the world. The Bear was beaten. This was a perfect weapon to inflict emotional grief on the Russians without endangering Americans. Then things became complicated and unraveled. An agreement, unknown to the public, had been made during the war with the Mujahideen. America promised the Mujahideen would be given control of Afghanistan after defeating Russia. This promise motivated harsher battles as more lives were sacrificed to defeat Russia and seize control of Afghanistan. After the defeat of Russia, America broke the promise to turn Afghanistan over to the Mujahideen. We immediately created an ad hoc political structure and ignored the promise and the countless lives the freedom fighters had sacrificed. However, their blood would not be sacrificed in vain. Their deaths became the motivation for a new Jihad, not against Russia, but against America. The mentality of revenge drove Osama bin Laden, and those scorned by lies and deceit, to fight against Americans who had once supported them. In 1993, the war led by Osama bin Laden began with the unsuccessful underground bombing of the *World Trade*

Center. Eight years later, bin Laden would show the world his tenacity and his fearless leadership by ordering a second attack on 09/11/2001.

The location? The World Trade Center.

This attack was successful as jets, full of innocent people and fuel, impacted each tower, engulfing them in flames. The beginning of the end ensued as both buildings collapsed into heaps of concrete, steel, and dust. The symbol of American capitalism had become a ravaged remnant of revenge. In the attack's wake, another golden egg for the *Military Industrial Complex* presented itself. A new war had begun, and the MIC was in full operation with 100% citizen support as the *Cold War* was replaced by the *War on Terrorism*."

Bobby was shaking his head. "Yep! We fought that war for 20 years and still ended up surrendering Afghanistan with a huge present of military weapons that will be used against us. We could have saved billions of dollars and uncounted lives if our political elitists had kept their promise with Bin Laden."

"Ironic, isn't it? Now, the unfortunate twist of our *War on Terrorism*. The *Patriot Act*. Passed on October 26, 2001, gave the United States government, all those lawyers, extended powers to search foreigners' private emails, finances, and personal lives. The caveat to this was American citizens, who were not lawyers, failed to realize they were in the same boat and not exempt from illegal government searches and intrusions either."

Martinez asked. "How do we know Americans were spied on?"

"Thank Mr. Snowden, former NSA contractor, for sharing that information. He released information on the Internet via a person named Julian Assange. Now, years later, these two men live in exile as the United States government continues to fight for their extradition and arrest. Assange is living at the Ecuadorian embassy in London and has filed court cases against his arrest warrants issued by the UK. Snowden lives in Russia as a citizen and will never be turned over to America. As more information was released about illegal spying on Americans, investigators discovered the FBI has a computer program, *Carnivore*, capable of searching one million emails per hour. FBI managers said the program was used to search emails of people being investigated for criminal activity. Citizens quickly responded and voiced concern that few criminals outside of huge corporations and governments had more than a million emails. Why would a program of this nature be justified by the FBI? Simple. They actively search private emails."

Bobby raised his hands. "If we know the FBI illegally uses *Carnivore* to search email accounts, what protection do we have?"

"None, and it gets worse. The more I dug into these questionable activities, the more I discovered. Currently, there is a bill, *Restrict Act (S.686)*, commonly referred to the *Patriot Act 2.0*, that is proposed to protect Americans against illegal surveillance from foreign and domestic entities. The headliner and motivation for the creation of this bill is the Chinese owned company *TikTok*. Lawmakers accuse *TikTok* of using illegal surveillance to get information about every user. Interestingly, the *Restrict Act* never uses the term *TikTok* in the document. If this bill is passed into law, the protection from illegal foreign and domestic surveillance will not include our federal government. This is another tool used to promote the philosophy of lawless political factions and their ability to silence anyone who disagrees. This was proven when Elon Musk released the *Twitter* records showing illegal FBI and government intrusion and control of user accounts, which further revealed other illegal operation and oversight of *Facebook* accounts. We have wars outside of our borders. Unfortunately, the wars inside our borders are more destructive and more critical.

This is where we are today. Unfortunately, my philosophy and threat to reveal these truths to the public were not appreciated by our prolific elitists in the government. Which is why I became an immediate threat, resulting in my detainment on the 6th floor, with the collective hope from many I would die in obscurity. I was not fighting against people; I was fighting a philosophy of greed driven by a faction of politicians and their cronies that skirted accountability, believing they are above the law. Fortunately, I escaped and am here fighting with other like-minded factions as hired guns continue to seek my documents and demise. As noted, we have lost most of our protection against illegal searches, warrantless arrests, and electronic eavesdropping."

"Unfortunately, the criminals who walk the halls of the Capital and Whitehouse continue to promote their evil."

Bobby was obviously angered. "What the heck! I'm with you! We must stop this!"

Albright nodded. "There is more evidence of these crimes, but I will stop here. It's almost 10:00 pm, and we will continue this topic later when the opportunity arises. Tomorrow, report to your regular duties. I will be in touch. Sheppard and I have some important issues to address." Bobby and Martinez arose, shook the hands of each man, and excused themselves.

GONE - Chapter 29

Marty was refreshed after showering and eating a bowl of chilled fruit when she fell asleep on the couch while reading. Bobby's call startled her into consciousness. He told her he would stop by after dropping Martinez off. He said he would arrive in about 20 minutes. She asked if he was hungry and wanted something to eat. He told her to relax and that he would check the kitchen when he arrived. Marty knew Bobby would arrive on time, knock, then open the door. Sure enough, 20 minutes later, there was a knock on the door. She opened the door and greeted him with her signature smile. Unfortunately, Bobby was not standing before her. She felt her body stiffen as she looked straight into the barrel of a suppressed pistol and then gazed into the menacing eyes of the masked intruder. He grabbed her by the arm and immediately turned her around. His accomplice taped her mouth before she could even scream, put handcuffs on her wrists, and placed a black cloth bag over her head. They grabbed her arms and quickly disappeared into the stairwell. One minute later, Bobby walked a few feet from the elevator to her room.

The door was cracked open.

He stepped in, expecting to see her reclining on the couch. He entered. She wasn't on the couch. He called her name. Nothing. Maybe she went to get some ice or was in the bathroom. He closed the door and walked into the kitchen. The documents were on the table. He searched the refrigerator and found some fresh apples and a bottle of cold water. He had to look at what she was so excited about sharing. He quickly scanned a few pages. She was meticulous. He chuckled, thinking she could have been Albright's child by her mannerisms and OCD episodes.

After a few minutes, he became concerned. His gut feeling was coming alive. He called her from his cell phone and heard her phone ringing in the bedroom. He explored the rooms and found nothing. She wasn't here. He went into the hall and walked to the ice machine, the laundry room, and the vending machines. Nothing! His mind switched to high gear. Something was not right. He quickly took the stairs to the front desk to see if she was there. The concierge assured him Marty had not stopped by.

"No, sir. I saw her earlier in the day. I noticed she had arrived earlier than usual. Sometime around 2:00 pm."

Bobby scanned the lobby. "Thank you. I appreciate your help. If she stops by, will you tell her Colonel Arrollos is trying to contact her?" Bobby handed the man a business card.

"Of course."

He ran up the stairs to her room and looked around for any details that might provide information. The first thing he noticed was her shoes next to the door. She never left the room without shoes. He looked into the hallway. Next to the door frame, he found an earring. It may have fallen off, but without her shoes, this showed she may have struggled and been abducted. He walked to the couch and looked around the room for any hints of anything else. The fatigue of a long day quickly vanished. He felt his stomach continue to tighten. Marty's purse was on the floor next to the couch. He quickly rifled through it. Her keys and wallet were there. Something was wrong.

Marty was rushed from the building and put into a vehicle outside the parking area. It seemed to be a van or SUV of some sort, judging by the space when she was shoved in. They sat for a few minutes while someone in the vehicle made a phone call. She couldn't understand the conversation. After the call, the sounds of squealing tires filled the air as the driver performed a hard turn and sped away. The force of the turn tossed her into the left side of the interior. She decided it was best to stay down. This would help her avoid other turns and the possibility of hard contact with the interior walls of the vehicle during the trip. As they traveled, she listened intently for the distinctive sounds of trains, trucks, boats, bells, sirens, or other telltale noises while taking in the odors along the route.

Albright was shocked that Bobby interrupted his meeting with Sheppard. However, he knew the call would have to be something urgent. As Bobby explained Marty had been abducted, Albright maintained his normal demeanor, subdued, replaced by a noticeable concern in his voice. Bobby filled in the gaps of what he saw while going floor-to-floor. Albright said he would get technology involved, his code phrase for black ops, and asked Bobby to get his FBI credentials and badge and begin reviewing video from the hotel and neighboring establishments that used security cameras. Bobby knew the badge would quickly open doors with the hotel manager without question. Reviewing the security videos should provide evidence of what happened to Marty.

The manager cooperated with Bobby.

Bobby returned to the front desk and identified himself as an FBI agent with an urgent situation. He explained that one of his partners had been kidnapped and was in immediate danger. He asked if it was possible to review the security video footage, hoping to identify anything that would help him find Marty. The manager immediately cooperated and took him to a secure office. They began reviewing each camera's data. The first camera showed a few cars entering the parking area and a white utility van branded "*Hotel Fixes*." Bobby asked the manager if he had used *Hotel Fixes* for any maintenance or services. The Manager said he had never heard of them. Bobby took a chance and focused his attention on the van. After viewing three of the video systems, he saw two hooded men, from different perspectives, wearing masks, exit the van and return in less than two minutes with Marty between them. They put her in the back of the vehicle. After sitting for a minute or two, they sped off the property. The driver was the only person who could be seen. The van exited, turned right, and traveled north. Bobby got the license plate number and texted it to Albright. Two minutes later, while still reviewing the videos, Albright responded that the number was a numeric acrostic that translated into "Sorry." An altered paper dealer plate was used to keep the cops at bay.

Bobby was frantic, as he was thinking about Marty's safety. It was consuming his attention and emotions while dictating his determination to find her. Their relationship as friends was close, very close. He had developed feelings for her he never shared, especially after the night of the shooting. Albright was busy contacting the Black Ops specialists. These guys were connected on every surveillance front; pedestrian cameras around the city with facial recognition software, drones that provided aerial surveillance of the area's entire area, and traffic recordings that would have anything about the vehicle. The dragnet had been cast and they would have to wait until the van was located.

―――――――

Marty sat in the back of the van, not knowing where she was or where she was headed. Twenty minutes later, the van stopped, the door opened, and she was taken to another vehicle. Bobby continued into the night visiting different businesses in search of clues, one at a time, trying to track the van. He promised himself that he would walk the streets and talk to everyone to find Marty. Albright called Bobby and told him the enhanced video revealed verified the paper license plate, the same number, and the driver who wore sunglasses and a baseball cap with no logo. At this point, it was impossible to determine anything about the driver. At 0300, Bobby returned to Marty's room. If she escaped, this would be the place where she would return. Her captors would know that too, allowing Bobby time to inflict some serious pain upon them. His hope of confronting them vanished as Albright's text to meet at the Smithsonian at 0700 interrupted. That would give him about three hours of sleep. He had no answers, no clues, and no energy. He was drained. In a city that never slept, Bobby fell into a deep sleep with his hand holding a Sig Sauer P220. He was proactive. At 0600, he fought off the exhaustion and took a quick shower. As he thought about Marty, his adrenaline kicked in and he was focused on Marty while driving to meet Albright. Both men arrived at the parking garage almost simultaneously. They walked together, talking about the situation and the potential scenarios to get Marty. When they arrived at the office entrance, Albright quickly stopped Bobby with his left arm and pointed at the lock. Bobby immediately recognized a forced breach from a suppressed weapon. Bobby stepped in front of Albright and removed his Sig from the pancake holster. He moved slowly, stealthily, as he visually inspected everything for anything. When they arrived at the vault, the door was ajar. Bobby motioned Albright to open the door while he sliced the pie. The term for a procedure used to make a visual inspection without showing yourself before entering a room or hallway. Albright hadn't moved the door six inches when Bobby realized why it was left open.

Someone left in a hurry.

Bobby made a hand motion. "Stop. Now we know why the door was breached, and this one left open. Somebody made a quick entry and exit after doing business."

Albright peeked around the door. His eyes widened as he looked at the dead bodies of the goons, each lying face down, surrounded by a crimson pool of blood caused by a single shot to the back of the head. Albright slowly stepped into the vault with Bobby next to him. DeLorean and Kuka were still secured in the chairs. Their faces were bloody, eyes swollen, and lips split. Somebody wanted information, and they took a set of brass knuckles to them to get whatever they came for. Unlike the goons, their throats had been slashed. One was probably killed before the other in this grotesque manner to get the information. Bobby looked at their pale bodies, feeling mixed emotions. This was no way for any of these people to die. Whoever did this was on a mission, not a random holdup by a street punk. This had all the earmarking of a military snatch-and-grab operation. Bobby knew DeLorean would never allow his sister to die alone. They lived, worked, and died together without saying a word. Hopefully, silence was their greatest and final act of defiance. As Bobby surveyed the carnage, Albright was on the phone.

He hung up. "We need to get out of here now. I have a cleaner on the way with his team. They will be finished by noon."

Bobby was angry, wondering if the people who did this were the ones who had taken Marty. Albright put his hand on Bobby's shoulder. "We will get the people who did this. I promise you. Now let's get out of here."

THE HUNT BEGINS - Chapter 30

As the adrenaline waned, Bobby felt exhaustion rekindling itself. He was tired. They had quickly left the *Smithsonian* and went their separate ways in case they were followed. Albright told Bobby his resources were looking into the events that led to Marty's kidnapping and the killings. The items on their plate were growing. Albright then informed Bobby that he would contact him immediately when he received information about either incident. After arriving at his home away from home, Bobby left the ringer on, changed into a T-shirt and shorts, then fell asleep and slept well. When he awoke, he was confused. The deep sleep, coupled with the events, put him into a mental fog. After a few minutes, he collected his faculties and picked up his phone to call Marty. When prompted to leave a voice message, he sobered quickly, remembering that the morning ritual had taken an unexpected twist with her disappearance. He checked his text messages. Nothing. He checked his email. Nothing. Was Albright sincere about finding answers or giving him false hope? He repeated the events of Marty's kidnapping in his head when the ring of the cell phone interrupted his train of thought.

He quickly answered the phone.

Albright told him there might be a break in the case and to go to a park in Rockville. Bobby acknowledged and told Albright he was en route. He went to the sink, splashed some water on his face, combed his matted hair, put a stick of gum in his mouth, secured his FBI credentials, and holstered his pistol. After putting on his shoes, he went out the door and drove to the park. He arrived 15 minutes later and was shocked to see the smoldering remains of the van with police cars, fire trucks, and an ambulance cordoned off with yellow crime scene tape. As he walked toward the van, he was stopped by a police officer. He flashed his badge and kneeled under the crime scene tape to pass, then walked to the coroner, who was closing a body bag atop a gurney. Bobby reached out with his hand as his heart sank. "Stop! Is that a female?"

The coroner turned to him. "Can I help you?"

For the second time in 30 seconds, Bobby flashed his credentials. "Yes. Are those the remains of a female?"

"I don't know."

Something didn't register with Bobby. "I'm sorry. You don't know if that's a female in the body bag?"

The coroner looked directly at him. "In most cases, I could answer your question, agent. Unfortunately, this body has no hands, no feet, no teeth, no brain, and has been burned into a cinder. I've never seen a body covered with gasoline both outside and inside before igniting it. Somebody wanted to send a message and ensure there was no evidence. They knew exactly what they were doing. The coroner unzipped the bag and opened it like a taco. Bobby had seen the effects of combat from incineration weapons, and the skeleton was a reminder of those gruesome moments. The skin was charred off with bones, burned white from the heat, exposing an awkward array of strewed remains."

Bobby lowered his head and clenched his fist tightly. He was angry. "Thank you."

"I will try to ID the victim and distribute the results to local and federal law enforcement agencies. This case could land itself in either jurisdiction."

"I, we, will have to wait and see what you discover. Thank you."

The coroner nodded. "I will do my best, but in all honesty, it doesn't look promising. Please excuse me."

Bobby nodded and walked to the car. Each step was heavy with emotion. He knew once he sat inside the car, his emotions would take over. And just as he surmised, he wept after the door was closed. He pounded his palms on the steering wheel. He hadn't cried this hard since Afghanistan when he sent the bodies of his brave comrade's homes with letters to each of their families. As he cried, he texted Albright a message between tears. He told Albright they would meet later because he needed some alone time. His eyes ached, and his head hurt. He was crushed, thinking that Marty could have died in such a horrible manner. After He drove to the hotel, showered, prayed, and fell asleep crying.

Albright had intentionally stayed away from the park. He knew this discovery would be an emotional time for Bobby. His law enforcement source had called and provided the grisly details regarding the crime scene and the condition of the victim. Albright had enough drama for the time being. He continued to sit in silence while reviewing the evidence of Marty's abduction. He knew someone was getting close to the team. For almost seven decades, he stealthily managed his activities in silence and obscurity.

Now, in the blink of an eye, everything he was disclosed.

He would contact Bobby later because more urgent matters were upon him. His fear of being captured manifested his determination to survive. He reflected on the targeted assassination attempt of Bobby a week ago, and now Marty was missing. This was no coincidence. Someone, or possibly more than one, was actively involved in finding him and the documents. They knew precisely where Marty lived and worked. They targeted Bobby. Now he would be the next. He was perplexed initially and put the pieces of the puzzle together. The information about Marty, Bobby, and himself was classified. For that information to get released to hostiles, foreign or domestic, someone had to leak information. The first piece of the puzzle was protecting themselves, which had failed because of a situation outside their control; they had been compromised. The second, locate and identify the threat. DeLorean and Kuku were history. They had been permanently removed from the equation after providing some valuable information. Sheppard had a way of getting people to talk, then disposing of them. Marty was missing and possibly killed. Bobby was currently incapable of thinking soundly because of emotional distractions and fatigue. The third, finding the leak, would also include discovering the remaining threat. Therefore, Albright was the lone wolf who started the process of discovery to eventually disclose the leak. He was back in the field, and he loved it. He hadn't felt this much adrenaline since his first mission to meet Churchill. He summoned Sheppard from the adjoining office and they left ready to engage their adversaries; those who hunted him would become the hunted.

TOOLS OF THE TRADE - Chapter 31

Bobby awoke several hours later. Still, overcome with emotions, he shelved the tears and replaced them with anger. The more he thought about Marty, the angrier he became, until he was consumed by a seething fire of retribution. He was in combat mode and looked at everyone as an aggressor. Little did he know, Albright had taken the hunter path, too. **With Marty taken hostage, Bobby had few options outside of waiting for Albright.**

Bobby texted Albright, "Anything?"

Albright responded. "Nothing yet. Relax. We are going to get this. Can you meet me at the office at 0900?"

Bobby needed clarity. "Your private office?"

"Yes. That one. See you there."

Bobby had over two hours before they would meet. He did fifteen minutes of calisthenics, showered, dressed, ate a toasted beagle, drank a *Monster*, and began phase one of his plan. Traffic was heavy as normal, but he drove the back streets to save time, which wouldn't delay his meeting with Albright. He stopped in front of the house. Carefully scanned the area, then backed the vehicle into the driveway. If anyone saw him and reported the tags to the police, it would return "official business government." He loved the fact of carrying an FBI credential with his photo and the name "Ivan M. Justice." He caught the humor of Albright when he realized his abbreviated name was "I. M. Justice." Irony and humor cross paths.

He hesitated several times before exiting the vehicle and deciding to enter. This was his covert operation to get the equipment and weapons needed to provide adequate protection if he was confronted. He knew Albright would have a cow, but that didn't matter because Marty was more important. Bobby was going outside the wire and if he compromised anything, Albright would have his head on a platter. However, with everything at stake, he went early instead of a late-at-night visit under the veil of darkness.

After scanning the area, he decided to enter through the front door.

He knew a front door exit would not attract attention. He exited the vehicle, took out the key, and entered. Everything he needed was in his house. Surprisingly, the house did not smell musty. The air conditioner was still on, which kept the moisture down while maintaining a constant temperature. He mentally thanked Albright. He hurried into the bedroom, rolled back the large floor rug, then removed a piece of the hardwood floor, exposing the dial of the combination lock and handle. In an instant, the tumblers fell into place as quickly as he rotated the dial.

He grabbed the flush-mounted handle and slid the door open. The flush-mounted sliding door gave him full access to everything. He removed three pre-packed duffle bags that contained several weapons that included suppressed automatic rifles, many loaded magazines, several flash-bang devices, two hand grenades, a claymore mine, two Sig P220 pistols, and tactical body armor with a Kevlar helmet. After placing the three duffle bags on the floor next to him, he removed a hard case that contained his *SIG716 DMR, 7.62 Semi-Auto Suppressed Sniper Rifle*. He was good to go. He put everything back in order, secured the door, and left.

Several miles always the alarm for the electronic monitoring equipment sounded. The sentry quickly reviewed the camera and engaged the recording system. He could see a lone person walking from the front door, through the living room, and into the bedroom. The surveillance system had been installed after the incident. Bobby had no clue he was being watched. The sentry picked up the phone and called Dr. Albright, then explained the details. Albright told the sentry to hold on. He put the sentry on hold and dialed a second number. Bobby had just turned onto the street, distancing himself from the house, when his cell phone interrupted. He looked at the caller ID. It was Albright. Hopefully, he had good news about Marty.

He answered. "Hello."

"It would have been much easier if you would have asked me to get weapons from your house. Actually, it would have been much better because you wouldn't be compromised. I'm sure you know by now I'm not happy."

Bobby felt like a toddler getting his butt chewed out by an angry parent before they whipped his behind. Bobby steeled himself. "I need these weapons. I assumed you would have denied my request to get them."

"You assumed correctly. It wasn't the weapons! As I said, we cannot risk compromising you! Your decision to do this surprised me. Remember, you were recently the target of a daylight assassination, and I cannot allow that to happen again. Until this moment, I've never second-guessed your decisions. Now get out of there and meet me in thirty minutes, as planned."

"Yes, sir." Bobby knew he messed up, but he would rather ask for forgiveness than leave Marty to the wolves. Thirty minutes later, he arrived at the office. Albright was already parked and waiting. Both men secured their vehicles and walked to the entrance. Albright had his signature stoic face and glared at Bobby, who smiled and nodded.

Albright opened the door, and both men entered. The system was secured before they walked to the office. Albright made his verbal announcement, and everything came to life. They sat in their respective seats.

Albright spoke first. "I know I will not have to speak with you about your error in judgment. Please keep every wild, hair-brained idea in check until you have spoken with me. Any questions?"

"None."

"Thank you. I needed to meet you in secret. There are some details of our operations that you must know as we move forward."

Bobby nodded. "I'm all ears."

"I have said you are being groomed for my position. At this point, especially with the complications caused by Marty's kidnapping, I must share some ugly aspects of your upcoming responsibilities."

"Thank you. But before we continue, may I ask a question?"

Albright nodded.

"Why did you and Sheppard kill DeLorean, Kuka, and the goons?"

Albright was surprised, but kept his composure. "What makes you think that?"

Bobby grinned. "Before Martinez and I left this office the other night, you remained with Sheppard to finish some additional issues. Early the following morning, you told me to meet you at the office. You needed an alibi and witnesses to attest you were in a meeting with three men and arrived early at the office for a meeting with me. Nice twist! You had me believing that we arrived at a crime scene, a murder, but after I thought about it, I realized you never took cover when I was clearing the rooms. Anyone who knew we could walk into a potential trap or crime scene would have done everything possible to stay safe. You walked down the corridor as if you owned it."

Albright smiled. "Well done! I won't say I did that on purpose, but you impress me with your keen situational awareness."

Bobby nodded. "Let me guess. You held the cloak of Sheppard while he did your dirty work? Sounds just like Saul holding the cloaks of everyone who stoned Stephen to death after he incited the killing. Would you define that as hypocritical?"

Albright wasn't impressed with the negativity. "Am I to assume you could do a better job? Remember, you are slotted for this position soon. You have been told some things, but you have not been told everything. If you think protecting our country against foreign and domestic threats is easy, you have another thing coming. I know you experienced combat and saw unimaginable horrors. Please remember, my duties are to be proactive, avoid war, not reactive."

"Did they talk?"

Albright was surprised. "What? Did who talk?"

"DeLorean and Kuka, when you were beating them to death. Did they say anything or was this your opportunity to get even with DeLorean for putting you on the 6th floor?"

"I did no such thing! DeLorean and Kuka have been in spying and double agent work for years. They followed in the footsteps of their grandfather. He loved to kill and had a passion for jumping ship to the country that paid the best for his experience and services. He was from Finland and ended up dying in Vietnam as a Green Beret."

Now Bobby was surprised. "Finland? A Green Beret? Was he killed in a helicopter crash?"

Albright looked perplexed. "Yes. How would you know that?"

"Lauri Allan Törni began his military career as a soldier in the Finnish army fighting the Soviets in World War II. After Finland defeated the Soviets, he joined Germany as an SS officer so he could continue killing the Soviets. After the war, he came to America, changed his name to Larry Thorne, and joined the Green Beret. His battlefield experience was immediately recognized and embraced. He was sent to Officer Candidate School (OCS) and promoted to officer, where he created and taught several training programs used by the Green Beret. He was killed in a helicopter crash in Vietnam. The 46-year-old is buried at *Arlington National Cemetery*. He was fearless. He earned a Bronze Star and two Purple Hearts."

Albright shook his head. "I'm impressed, but why would you know the details of this man?"

"I have a photo of him on the wall in my office. My mother was a Finn, and as a Finn, I was intrigued by Finland and researched various areas of its culture. I also have a photo of Simo Häyhä, the greatest sniper to have ever lived. He had over 505 kills using a rifle that is nothing like those issued today. I can't image how many kills he would have had using modern weapons."

"I've never met anyone from Finland outside of my political exploits. It's good to know your passions are well-directed. You will be a perfect addition to this unit. By the way, I have a piece of trivia for you. Did you know that Winston Churchill was an American citizen? Your trivia about Larry Thorne reminded me."

"That is very interesting. What I am about to tell you is very interesting too. I'm having second thoughts. What can you tell me that will erase the murder of DeLorean and his sister from my mind? By the way, you haven't answered my first question."

"DeLorean was attached to a top-secret unit, similar to my assignment. He was ordered to protect the nation from domestic threats. After passaging the *Patriot Act*, he could use whatever resources necessary, including those that violated the 4th Amendment, to get information on anyone considered a threat to national security."

"Sounds like the philosophy of J. Edgar Hoover. He used the FBI as his spy network to get information on several high-profile people, including the Kennedys."

"Initially, the operations went smoothly. Then, after a few years in the sandbox, legislators wanted more accountability as foreign nationals who worked with, and supported us, moved to America. Even though they had put their lives on the line, the DC elite did not trust them. Over time, the overarching reach of DeLorean's department included former and retired intelligence personnel. I felt this went way beyond the authority defined in the *Patriot Act*. I voiced my concerns to the Whitehouse and was told to mind my own business and stay in my lane. When I retired, I never imagined that my comments regarding the protection of our intelligence personnel had put the administration on edge. This concern for others led to my incarceration on the 6th floor where I was supposed to die. I had to send a message to Washington. Ending DeLorean and his sister's involvement was the only way they would understand I am aware of what is happening."

"So, you use the 'greater good' as the foundation to murder DeLorean and his sister? I could say they deserved it, or that karma is a terrible thing. Regardless, I appreciate your explanation. What about the goons? Did you have to murder them, too?"

"They will be reported as rogue military members who took justice into their own hands. One of them is the grandson of a man who was imprisoned on the 6th floor and later released when my escape I spilled the beans. He had a reason to kill DeLorean because of what they did to his grandfather."

Bobby sighed. "The price we pay for freedom and the perception of it."

"Exactly, now let me fill you in on some other details of my duties that you will inherit."

There was a knock on the door. "Come in." He pivoted his chair from the window back to his desk. "What do you have for me?"

"Sir, for two days we have been attempting to contact LTC DeLorean and have been unsuccessful. His NCOIC informed us he would be engaged in a top-secret operation with a member of the Finnish Embassy to get information on a high-profile former operator. He hasn't been seen or heard from since then."

"Do you think this is a problem for us?"

"Sir. If this has anything to do with your quest to find this former operator, it could cause some major issues if the people on the other side of the aisle find out."

"I'm not worried about anyone from either side of the aisle. Everyone is involved. They will keep their mouths shut! Stay on this and keep me informed."

"I will. Excuse me."

He watched the attaché exit the office, then turned his chair and attention to the birds soaring gracefully in the air, oblivious to the problems he was facing.

NEW RULES - Chapter 32

Everything was falling into place perfectly. The collateral assets had been collected and the next phase of the operation would begin today, actually, right now. He sat up in his chair, smiled devilishly, and picked up the cell phone. After pressing the speed dial, there was an immediate answer.

"Hello."

"Good morning. I hope this call finds you in good spirits. How are you today?"

"I'm well. What do you want?"

The devilish smile widened as he provoked the listener. "Why such a negative attitude? Did you eat breakfast? Are you hangry?"

"Neither. I have more important issues to attend to. Now hurry along. What do you want?"

"Why do you banter with me? You know why I called. Do you have the asset information for me? I have a team ready to pick up the property."

There was silence. Then the sound of someone with a tone of sharpness in their words. "I have a problem."

"Really? What that might be?"

"The head of the operations group is missing. We haven't heard from him in two days. I have another team activated and their mission is to locate him. We cannot afford for his information to be shared. That would compromise everything. If that happens, I will not go down alone. Do you understand?"

He laughed at the attempted threat. It did not intimidate him. "Your words seem so strong, yet there is an air of fear in your voice. Why? Because your administration is weak, and the entire world knows it. You have lost all credibility as a leader and person. You are a washed-up politician who has passed his time of functional purpose. You should resign and save face while you can.

Unfortunately, you know the Vice-President is inept, and putting that person into the Oval Office would further tarnish your character, if that is even possible at this point! Please refrain from your vain attempts to push back. You are already defeated. Accept your situation."

"You are not talking to one of your subordinates." His voice raised. "You are talking to the President of the United States!"

The Aristocrat was done with childish bantering.

The Aristocrat shouted back. "Shut up! You are in no position to question who I am. You are nothing but a political pawn used by your party to promote its agenda and mine. You are nothing but a puppet for them and me! Did you hear me? A puppet! You have been emasculated before the entire world. Now, when will I get my information?"

His voice lowered. He cowered before the Aristocrat in the same manner many world leaders had. "I told you the head of that operations group is missing. I am doing everything possible to locate him."

His eyes furrowed. "I need to know the status by noon. If you haven't resolved the situation by that time, I will start my second plan. Do you understand the gravity of my words?"

"Yes. I will contact you no later than noon."

The president turned his chair to the window and continued watching the birds. This was his only purpose since relinquishing his power as president to his party and the Aristocrat. He knew the words were true. He was emasculated before the world. He was a puppet. He would be known as the worst president in history. He watched the birds soar gracefully in their peaceful arena above the ocean of humanity, thick with political pollution.

The Aristocrat had hung up and pressed another number on the speed dial. "Good morning. How can I be of assistance?"

The Aristocrat loved the respect and promptness given to him by his subordinates, especially the Commander. "Good morning, Commander. I called to give you a head-up regarding the next phase in our operations. I just got off the phone with that inept American."

The Commander interrupted. "Sir, which one? They are all inept, so please enlighten me."

The furrow on his forehead disappeared as he laughed. "I needed some humor. Thank you. Perfect timing."

The Commander continued. "I am in awe as America collapses from within. They are so consumed with pleasing everyone they are forfeiting their core values, morals, and survival. No other country is regressing. They are the modern-day Romans, who had everything and lost everything. The once mighty empire is nothing today, as America dictates their demise."

The smile reappeared. "Exactly! That's what makes our purpose and mission so critical. Our once-feared world power is powerless! Once the dollar is reduced to worthless paper, America will cease to exist. Their time of printing worthless money will be over and so will their country. I cannot tell you how happy this makes me. I'm sorry I went down another path. Allow me to answer your question. I just finished talking to the biggest inept American, the President, and he advised me their head of operations is missing. Seems he has been missing for two days. My guess is he probably defected to another country and got out before the end."

Now the Commander laughed. "How insane is this? We would never have had this conversation about America a few years ago. It seems our mission to indoctrinate the children has come to fruition. Khrushchev was correct when he said, '*We will take America without firing a shot.*'"

The Aristocrat's eyes widened as the revelation of his rise to power manifested itself to further heights. "Who would have guessed that the mad Russian banging his shoe on the podium of the United Nations was clairvoyant?"

"I'm glad your father followed his mantra and united with Russia to supplant our agenda. We calculated it would take three generations before their youth would orchestrate our goals. They did it in two. Fear is a powerful tool. Getting them to surrender their weapons while they are distracted in appeasing everyone will make our invasion easy. I'm glad Stalin didn't have that mindset when Germany knocked on their door. If so, everybody would be speaking German."

The Aristocrat looked at his watch. "You don't have much time to prepare an alternate plan for the operation, but I know you are capable. Thank you for your diligence. I will call you when I get the information from the inept leader of America."

He grinned. "Yes, sir. I'm standing by."

The Aristocrat was not frustrated with the change of plans. The Commander's words were enlightening, perfect, and a reminder of their objectives. He sat back in his chair and smiled as he reflected on the words and mission to destroy America from within. It won't be long now.

CONTACT - Chapter 33

Albright concluded the details of what was required of Bobby as he groomed him for his position. Bobby looked at Albright. "Nothing on Marty?"

Albright shook his head. "No."

"Are you not concerned about her safety?"

Albright's eyes projected disdain that Bobby dared to ask a question of that nature. "I am concerned. You, however, are becoming negative and creating friction between us."

Bobby caught the tension in Albright's voice. "I hate waiting! I get frustrated."

It was as if orchestrated. Bobby's cell phone rang. The caller ID said, Unknown. "I need to answer this. I have that gut feeling something is about to happen."

Albright shrugged his shoulders. "Do it!"

Bobby answered the phone and put it on the speaker. "Colonel Arrollos?" Bobby muted the phone. "That's not Martin. He is the only person I've spoken with, and I don't recognize that voice."

Albright smiled. "Talk to him. Let's see where this goes. If it's a telemarketer, I will take them out myself."

Bobby smirked at Albright's humor. "Who is asking?"

"I am a person, a professional actually, like you, who has a situation."

Bobby and Albright shared a glance. "What type of situation?"

"One that requires Dr. Anderson Albright."

Albright's expression immediately changed.

"Who is Dr. Anderson Albright?"

"You know exactly who he is. He is the person who hired you and Marty Bell after he escaped the 6th floor."

Bobby muted the phone. "Whoever this is, they have access to confidential information."

Bobby unmuted the phone. "Who told you this?"

Bobby was shocked when he heard the voice. "Bobby, it's me, Marty. Don't do it! Don't do anything!"

"Does that answer your question? Seems your friend provided information when we used some enhanced questioning techniques on her."

Bobby seethed with anger, but kept his composure. "It seems you failed to realize our commitment to our jobs and country. We will sacrifice everything if necessary."

"I love the American's dedication to God and country. Your words of self-sacrifice to protect everyone are noted, but are you prepared to sacrifice more people?"

Bobby could hear some scuffling, then a muted voice, followed by the distinct sound of duct tape being ripped from someone's face. Another voice, a female, spoke. "They have us. All three of us."

Bobby tried to determine who was speaking and who she was talking about. "Who is this? Who do they have?"

"Angela! The nurse Marty replaced. They also have Little Blood. They are threatening to kill us if you don't cooperate. They want Dr. Albright and his documents."

The message was ominous, especially when the Aristocrat added his perspective. "Colonel, I hope your friends' pleas for their lives persuade you to take my demands seriously."

Albright took the phone from Bobby. "Who is this?"

The Aristocrat immediately distinguished the change in voices. "Well, what do we have here? The voice has changed, but the question remains the same. Let me put it so you will completely understand, Dr. Albright. I am a man fueled by my lust for power, which motivates me to use whatever means necessary to get what I want. I, like you, will never accept defeat. I know about you and the documents you penned. Those documents will give me power over the democratic nations that have hidden their crimes against humanity. Their graft. Their greed. Their malevolence. I am sure you can appreciate my passion for wanting them."

Albright was stoic. "If I agreed to surrender my documents to you, how am I to know you would not kill everyone? If you are a man who shares the same integrity and persona as me, I would expect no witnesses. Remember, dead men, tell no tales."

An evil grin appeared on the Aristocrat's face. "You have no guarantee. You would have to trust me."

Albright laughed. "Trust you? What a joke! You can do whatever you want with the three hostages." Bobby's expression reflected ferocity. "You know the rule of war and terrorism. Never negotiate with a terrorist. I guess that concludes this call. Goodbye."

The Aristocrat was shocked. His tactics of threatening to kill innocent people always got him what he wanted. Albright's terse response put him in a position of urgent negotiation. "Hold on Dr. Albright. I am not a cold-blooded murderer, as you think. I am a professional with an agenda and you possess something I need. In fact, you possess the only remaining item I need to put me in a position of total control. If I guaranteed that your friends and you would never be harmed, would you consider making the exchange of three people for one set of documents?"

Albright grinned. Not a grin of humor. A grin of evil, sinister to be exact. Something Bobby had never seen before. "We meet at my location, at my time. At my discretion. Is that clear?"

"Clear. How and where do you want me to meet you?"

"Get a pen and paper ready to note the location." The Aristocrat was at his desk. Writing instruments costing thousands of dollars were at his disposal. "I'm ready."

"At 1330, you will drive and meet a lone man wearing a *Green Bay Packers* hat at the steps of the entrance at to 2 Montgomery Avenue. He will give you a sealed envelope. The address of our meeting location will be enclosed. Immediately drive to the location. It should take you 35 minutes. Any longer than that and I walk. Do you understand?"

"Yes. I will do as you request. We meet tomorrow."

Albright nodded. "We do!" Then he hung up the phone.

Bobby was in awe. He was a ball of emotions. Three of his friends were held hostage by a madman who would meet with Albright tomorrow for the exchange. His thoughts were interrupted by Albright. "Are you with me on this?"

Bobby nodded. "Yes."

"Then let's get ready for the meeting."

ONE CHANCE - Chapter 34

The covert operation and meeting would involve Albright, Marty, Angela, Little Blood, Bobby, and the Aristocrat. However, Albright and Bobby knew the Aristocrat would have a security detail close by in case something went south, or he wanted to ensure there were no witnesses. Either way, Albright knew he must control the situation. With help from Bobby and Sheppard, they outlined a plan after considering several potential scenarios. Sheppard, who was staying on site, would prepare coffee and snacks for the meeting. During the meeting, Bobby was impressed with Sheppard's keen sense of tactical awareness and proactive countermeasure perspectives. What caught Bobby's attention was the shared skills and insight Albright provided. Something did not mesh. Albright always said he was the special attaché for several presidential administrations, but here he displayed a military mentality normally evidenced by War College graduates, of which he was one. Perhaps there was more to Albright than he revealed. They collectively agreed to a proactive countermeasure plan that ensured the best possible outcome. Afterward, Bobby went to get Martinez and take him to the location so they could prepare for the exchange. Sheppard and Albright stayed and outlined the finer details of the operation. With the Aristocrat agreeing to meet them in a friendly area, they would have the upper hand. However, nothing could be taken for granted.

After disconnecting with Albright, the Aristocrat called the Commander for a meeting in his office. The Commander arrived five minutes later. The Aristocrat shared the details and agreements from his conversation with Albright and the exchange, then asked the Commander for his perspectives.

"Sir, we will follow orders from someone we have never met, and end up in an area we know nothing about. I understand your passion to get these documents, but our first step is to identify the meeting location. What is at 2 West Montgomery Avenue in Rockville?" As he spoke the Commander took his cell phone and searched, then looked at the Aristocrat accompanied with a sigh. "It's the *Rockville Police Department!*"

The Aristocrat shifted in his chair. "What's Albright up to?"

"Obviously, he doesn't want any problems, since he chose a very secure location for the exchange and is flexing his muscles in our faces. Regardless, it doesn't matter. We have an objective to complete and afterward, you will begin your greatest achievement." After entertaining several scenarios, they agreed to have backup personnel accompany them and remain out of sight, but close enough to intervene and intercept if necessary.

The Aristocrat smiled. "Yes, a team outside of listening and visual range will be perfect. Get them assembled."

"Yes, sir. I will do exactly that!"

The Aristocrat grinned as his thoughts manifested a mental conversation between the two. "So, you think you are messing with my head? Not today, doctor. I admit you are a formidable opponent. Unfortunately for you, I will play by your rules until I have the papers. Then my team will kill everyone. You are a weak old man who is in over his head. You have never met a man of my character and prowess. No man will ever meet a man of my prowess!" The Aristocrat smiled.

The Commander recapped the mission. "Here is the game plan. You will drop me off short of the meeting point. I will keep in contact with the backup team as I search for and prepare a clear line-of-sight location outside the perimeter. With my sniper rifle, I will monitor everything and keep you and the team advised. After you make the exchange, I will take out the trash, beginning with Albright. When you leave, pick me up and the backup team will escort us home."

"That sounds like a plan. As I mentioned earlier, I knew you would come up with a plan. Great job!" The Aristocrat arose and extended his hand as a gesture to show appreciation for a job well done. "Commander, I cannot tell you how much you have contributed to the mission, my success, and a New World Order. Thank you for everything."

"Sir, I am honored by your trust, admiration, and encouragement. This is the first of many dominoes that must fall, but with this, the others will follow accordingly. Thank you." With that, the Commander left to complete his tasks. The Aristocrat sat as the evil grin appeared in direct alignment with his thoughts. My time is now moments away.

Almost as if synchronized, Bobby was considering his time and the passion he would unleash during the meeting. At that moment, he and the Aristocrat shared similar tactical objectives...terminate any threat with extreme prejudice.

As Bobby drove to get Martinez, he thought about the situation and his responsibility to protect his friends. He had insight into the location, which gave him time to consider which locations were tactically advantageous. Bobby arrived and met Martinez in the office and reviewed predictable scenarios while sharing the various considerations of observation and interaction that Albright drafted. This volatile situation could explode in seconds, and having Sheppard and Martinez would help maintain a strong proactive defense. Bobby's gut told him to expect the worse because they were pitted against an adversary who was well connected with military and political figures; all of whom wanted Albright dead and his papers in their possession.

Even though Bobby and Martinez were trained in combat and covert operations with front-line experience, an engagement of this nature, a rendezvous with a psychopath who thirsted for the blood of the weak, was new and required their utmost attention. Sheppard and Albright made their mentality abundantly clear, "Shoot first and ask questions later." The gnawing question was how many of the Aristocrat's specialists would wait on the perimeter to kill the hostages after the exchange. Bobby's stomach twisted, but he embraced the surge of adrenaline.

He trusted no person, especially terrorists, and psychopaths.

    As Bobby shared the perspective scenarios with Martinez, they agreed the team needed a tactical vehicle to quickly secure and remove the hostages from the free-fire zone. It could not be a heavily armored transport vehicle. It had to be light, nimble, and able to navigate on- and off-road terrain with ease. Martinez knew of the exact vehicle and suggested the *Scorpion DPV* (Desert Patrol Vehicle) used by the SEALs. Bobby agreed and contacted his Navy Spec-Op contemporaries, and after explaining the situation to the commander, he was given the authorization to procure one. The commander volunteered a team if needed, but Bobby declined because this unique domestic situation could not be compromised, and any additional military members would complicate the situation if it failed. They drove to the agreed exchange location and met two Seals who had brought two vehicles with different passenger configurations.

    Bobby chose the one with a larger storage capacity in the rear in case the hostages had to quickly jump in. Martinez took possession of the DPV and would drive to the secret office using back roads to avoid unnecessary interest from the public. Upon return, Bobby looked for the best place to establish high-ground observation with cover and a location where Martinez could station himself and the DPV out of sight. An hour later, both locations were selected. When Martinez arrived, they set up the needed camouflage, concealment, and cover for both locations.

Martinez was far enough away to be concealed, but close enough to evacuate the hostages quickly. Bobby had established himself in an abandoned room with broken windows. This would allow him to shoot from a chair with the rifle supported on a table several feet away from the windows; concealing him perfectly. He had a clear line of sight and could see the area without obstruction. Inside the office, Albright had copied 20 pages from his dossier, 10 for the front and 10 for the back that would sandwich the complete volume of *War and Peace* between them. Never knowing what to expect, he hoped the Aristocrat would only scan a few pages of the voluminous fake dossier. Bobby shared the locations where he and Martinez would be located with Albright and Sheppard. Sheppard responded with a narrative of his observation duties from the office, using the hidden cameras to detect any aggressors in the surrounding area and tree lines. Everyone understood their job. They were good to go.

The following morning, Bobby awoke in the abandoned room. He slept there to avoid detection in case their location was compromised by any of the political allies who supported the Aristocrat. Martinez slept on the ground near the *Scorpion DPV*. He shared the same thoughts as Bobby. Albright was still sleeping in a comfortable bed in the building and wouldn't rise for another two hours. He seemed oblivious to the dangers of the situation. Sheppard was in tactical mode. He arose early and paced the office for mental preparation. The waiting game had begun. Bobby made himself comfortable in the seat and began looking for locations that would conceal an enemy sniper. Martinez stayed on the ground, catching some cat naps. After awakening, Albright tested the communications system with Bobby, Martinez, and Sheppard. The frequency and scrambled signal worked perfectly. They were ready.

The Aristocrat, Commander, and escorts met and made a final review of their duties and expectations. Once satisfied everything was ready, they began their trek.

An hour later, the *Green Bay Packer* radioed Sheppard that the package had been delivered. Sheppard passed the information and advised the team the exchange would take place in less than 30 minutes. The Aristocrat and Commander sat silently in the front seats with the three hostages behind them. Nobody spoke. The Commander texted the escorts to ensure the hostages knew and heard nothing. They had arrived at the drop-off point as the Aristocrat stopped out of sight to let the Commander out. The escorts would stay back, parked until either notified to assist or depart the area. The Commander quickly exited and in less than five minutes had located and set himself in a position of tactical advantage. Before continuing, the Aristocrat called Bobby to confirm he was near and had the hostages. Bobby acknowledged the information and said that Albright was waiting. He advised the team the package would arrive in a minute, then relaxed as he scanned the road through the adjustable *Leupold Mark 5HD* variable power sniper scope. Albright had exited the building and stood next to the car. Bobby did another comm check. Everyone was good. Bobby saw the vehicle approaching and told Albright; everyone heard the message. Albright nodded. The *Land Rover* arrived and stopped about 50 feet from Albright.

Everything was in order.

The Aristocrat lowered the tinted driver's side window. Albright nodded. Bobby had a clear line of sight at the Aristocrat's head. He was engaged. Sheppard broke Bobby's concentration by advising him there was a heat signature approximately 400 yards to Bobby's one o'clock. Bobby quickly scanned the area and located the barrel and scope peeking out of the foliage. Bobby then returned his attention to the Aristocrat and Albright. The scope mounted on his rifle provided perfect observation of the distance sniper and the immediate area.

The Commander watched intently. Scanning the abandoned property for any threats. He spoke with the escort supervisor, keeping him updated on the situation that Albright was standing by a vehicle and the Aristocrat arrived. The supervisor had the team check their weapons and be prepared to engage if necessary. They waited in silence.

The tinted windows made it difficult for Bobby to see who or what was inside, but he eventually distinguished three people were in the backseat. Albright reached into the parked car, removed a large carrying case, and slowly walked toward the *Land Rover,* stopping about ten feet short. The Commander had Albright in his crosshairs and radioed everyone. The rear driver-side door opened, and the blindfolded hostages exited. They stood motionless next to the vehicle with their hands secured behind their backs as instructed. With the window down, Bobby had the Aristocrat in his crosshairs. He noted the physical details of the Aristocrat. His hair was groomed perfectly, clean-shaven, with sharp facial features, and was wearing an expressive suit coat. Bobby pressed his throat mic and told everyone the exchange should happen soon. Albright nodded, Martinez was prepared, and Sheppard continued scanning the area for other hostiles. The Commander realized that the Land Rover was parked at an angle prohibiting him from seeing all the hostages.

The Aristocrat spoke. "Are all the documents in the case?"

Albright nodded. "Everything you want is here."

The Aristocrat grinned. "How do I know you are telling the truth?" Then he extended and aimed a pistol at

Albright. Bobby immediately felt his finger tense against the trigger, but stopped short of firing.

Albright smiled. "Do you think I want to do this again? At my age, I should be sitting in front of a television watching infomercials instead of standing here with a madman who has a pistol aimed at my head."

The Aristocrat smiled. "I see you have a sense of humor with a sarcastic flare, doctor. Let's hope you are forthright and have provided everything I told you to bring. If not, your future of watching infomercials will be cut short as well as the people you came to save."

Bobby could see Marty, Angela, and Little Blood. They were blindfolded, with their arms behind them secured with flex cuffs. Fortunately, they had shoes on their feet. One of the first things Bobby did when securing prisoners of war was to remove their shoes. It was difficult for them to run, and they could be quickly recaptured. They were defenseless but seemed unharmed. Bobby relayed the information. Martinez secured the wire cutters so he could quickly cut and removed the cuffs. With two weapons in the picture, Bobby knew both were focused on Albright. Bobby knew there would be several variables during the exchange. He prayed for the best and expected the worst. He was focused on the Aristocrat, who was talking to Albright.

With the hostages standing outside the vehicle, Bobby did not have a clean shot. He had to make a decision. He continued to focus on the Aristocrat. The sniper could kill the Albright and the hostages, but distance was on Bobby's side.

Bobby spoke into the radio. "Albright, you have two guns on you. The one directly in your face, and another at your eleven a few hundred yards out. When I tell you to drop, immediately fall to the ground." Bobby gave the cue and Albright began swinging the case back and forth in front of him, similar to what a hypnotist does with a watch. The Aristocrat and Commander both watched and questioned the motive. Their focus on the Aristocrat worked perfectly as Martinez appeared in a flash and came to an abrupt stop behind the *Land Rover's* left rear bumper. The Aristocrat reversed and crashed into the DPV tire like a bumper car. Martinez exited and quickly removed the blindfolds, cut the flex cuffs, and told the hostages to follow him. He ran to the driver's side and pushed each hostage into the rear area, then sped away. The Commander saw nothing but knew something was happening. He ordered the escorts to get here ASAP. The Supervisor told the team to ready their weapons and hang on. The Aristocrat could not expose himself to shoot the hostages, knowing he would be killed immediately if he took his weapon off Albright, which would keep the sniper in check. The Commander could hear the escort vehicle approaching but could do nothing except watch. Martinez got everyone into the DPV and was gone in seconds. With a pointed pistol at Albright, the Aristocrat told him to bring the case.

Albright walked the final ten feet and handed him the case.

The Aristocrat took the case and kept aim at Albright. Bobby ordered Albright to drop and as he fell, the Aristocrat squeezed the trigger twice. The first bullet grazed Albright's head, and the second missed entirely. Bobby had already aligned and acquired a sight picture of the moving Aristocrat who threw the case and took two shots at Albright. Bobby squeezed the trigger, and the recoil of the round was noticeable as the suppressed bullet made its way toward the Aristocrat's face. Upon impact, the flesh contorted splattered blood as the bullet passed cleanly through the soft tissue of the cheeks. Bobby saw bleeding from his left cheek as he slumped down on the steering wheel. Bobby also saw blood splatter on the inside of the windshield and dashboard. He knew the bullet had exited. Sheppard relayed a vehicle was quickly approaching. Bobby fixed and steadied his sight picture on the road as the vehicle approached. Bobby established a target acquisition of the driver's head and pulled the trigger. He watched the head explode, and the body sit lifelessly behind the wheel. Bobby noticed that the soldier behind him was covered in blood and dead, too. The round had passed through the head of the driver and hit the rear passenger in the throat. Bobby savored the two-for-one shot but concentrated on the passenger attempting to grab the steering wheel of the out-of-control vehicle. As he reached across to grab the steering wheel, the bullet hit his heart and he dropped out of sight. Bobby finished the remaining passenger with a headshot. Bobby had exacted his execution in less than ten seconds. The vehicle continued its course until impacting a tree and bursting into flames. In that moment, the Aristocrat raised his head and slammed the accelerator to the floor. He quickly sped away. The Commander had seen everything and was shocked that he could not help his team. He jumped up and ran toward the road. As he exited the woods and approached the edge of the road, his head exploded.

He fell dead on the blacktop.

The Aristocrat did not bother stopping or slowing. He saw the Commander fall and continued to speed away as the front right tire crushed the Commander's skull. Bobby had caught the motion of the Commander running toward the road and before he could squeeze the trigger, the Commander had taken a header and fall lifeless to the road. He looked out the window and saw Sheppard standing with a sniper rifle in hand. Bobby was in awe. Sheppard had just taken a four-hundred-yard shot at a moving target from a standing position, hitting the head. That killing skill was reserved for a select few. Bobby resumed his scan of the area with Sheppard, looking for additional threats. Albright was dazed as blood flowed into his right eye. He stood and wiped the blood away with his left palm. The moment was surreal.

The Aristocrat removed the silk handkerchief from his vest pocket. He placed it over the right cheek, trying to stop the flow of blood as he frantically veered left and right. His profanity was suppressed by the blood in his mouth, to a reduced series of gurgling sounds. Once he was safe and knew he wasn't being followed, he pulled over, removed the handkerchief, and looked into the mirror. He was shocked to see the gaping hole in his right cheek surrounded by shards of hanging flesh. Blood continued to flow onto his suit. His anger seethed, which subdued the pain of the wound. If the bullet had impacted an inch backward, his jaw and face would be gone, and his life would have ended immediately. As bad as this was, he knew soft tissue wounds healed quickly. Unfortunately, it would leave him scarred for life, but alive. He texted his medical staff, advising them he had facial entrance and exit wounds and required immediate attention. The response was quick and told him where to meet. Ten minutes later, he was sitting in the plush living room at his doctor's home in a recliner surrounded by a medical team tending to his wounds. Later, he would experience insult to injury when he discovered the papers in the case were useless and that Albright had won that battle. He assured himself the next encounter would end differently…it would end Albright's reign of power and promote his unabated rise to power. He never thought of the Commander again, just his replacement.

Albright told Sheppard to have everyone muster in the main room for a post-event debriefing. Before he entered, he went to the medical station. Martinez drove to the entrance and escorted the former hostages into the building. Marty and Angela had tear stains on their faces while Little Blood showed no emotion as they passed Sheppard, oblivious of his presence. They were still reeling from the immensity of the events and stared into nothingness. Life and death situations take people immediately out of their comfort zone and incarceration removed their fundamental flight-or-flight option of survival. They were mentally depleted. It would take a few days before they regained some peace of mind and a few weeks before returning to their "new" normal. Martinez escorted them to the kitchen for food and drink, a distraction to start them down the path of healing. Sheppard continued to scan the area as Bobby returned from his temporary Eagle's Nest. Ironic how this code name during this operation was also used at his former location in Rockville. Before entering the building, he locked eyes with Sheppard, and without saying a word, each knew exactly what the other was thinking. The men of Spec-Ops shared a mental and emotional camaraderie that went beyond their culture, language, position, and allegiance; a mindset chiseled from the adrenaline of combat, sculpted in a forum few people ever experienced. They nodded and smiled.

Albright had washed the wound, dressed it, and washed the blood from his face. By the time he arrived, everyone was seated, some eating, but all thinking about the episode. Albright began by thanking everyone for their due diligence and reassured them they were fine. A few minutes later, the security system alerted everyone that a vehicle was parked outside the front door. Everyone tensed. Albright stood. "Relax. It is the escort to get Angela and Little Blood home. Sheppard left the room as Albright walked to Angela and extended his hand. He took it and arose. He hugged her. "I never thanked you for saving my life. You put yourself out there when I was destined to die in that bed on the 6fh floor. Today, you did it again. I can never thank you enough for what you did. You are my hero." Angela began to cry, then weep as the totality of everything was released. Albright held her as she wept in his arms. Everyone was silent.

Tears coursed down Marty's face.

Little Blood watched and nodded as he began crying. Their emotions had been tested and stretched to the limits; the healing process had begun. Martinez handed out paper towels. Angela sat then Albright walked to Little Blood, who stood as they hugged. "To you, I also owe my life. Your passion for video games was my key to getting access to your computer and contacting my rescuers. Thank you for your unknown contribution to saving me. I'm sorry each of you was taken into this unfortunate situation, but there is more to this than you will ever know or imagine. You do not know what you did and how many lives you saved." Everyone exchanged surprised glances.

Albright smiled. "On a pleasant note, Angela and Little Blood have received a sizeable amount of money deposited into their bank accounts. This should compensate both greatly for their sacrifices and dedication while ensuring they have comfortable lives. Thank you for your service." Sheppard entered with the escort.

Albright hugged them again. "Please go with this gentleman. He will take you home. You will never have contact with me again unless it requires your services, but I doubt that will be necessary. Thank you."

The escort motioned for them to follow. Marty jumped up and hugged each of them before they left. The tears continued. After they departed, Albright returned to his seat. "Well, now the fun begins."

For the second time in a minute, everyone looked surprised.

"This is our team. We have an important mission before us that will require more than you can imagine. I have assembled you specifically for this project to expose the effects of the *Inner Sanctum*. I will give you the details in two days. Today we begin a much-needed rest and recuperation. Bobby, you and Martinez will return the DPV and Sheppard will take you home. I will be for the day tidying up the loose ends of this operation and wait for the cleaning crew to arrive."

Everyone stood, shook hands, and left. Bobby joined Martinez in the drive to return the DPV. The air was refreshing and the drive pleasant. Martinez felt the vibration of his watch and read the message. "I NEED YOUR HELP. I HAVE NOBODY TO TURN TO. MY DAD AND AUNT HAVE BEEN MISSING FOR THREE DAYS. I'M FALLING APART. PLEASE HELP ME!"

Martinez was shocked. Bobby noticed the change in his expression. "Is everything ok?"

"No. I just received a text from Kiki, the waitress, that her father and aunt have been missing for three days. She said he is falling apart and needs my help."

Bobby did not expect her to contact Martinez, but remembered he shared his information at the restaurant. "What are you going to do?"

"I'm going to help her. What do you think happened?"

Bobby hated lying, but this was no time to be chivalrous and tell him her family had been murdered by his grandfather. "I don't know. Are you sure this is a good thing? After all, they are suspects in treasonous activities."

"I will help her. She needs someone."

After returning to the DPV, Bobby and Martinez joined Sheppard and took the ride home.

Albright texted a message. "EVERYTHING GOOD. OPERATION UNSUCCESSFUL. INFO SECURE. TEAM SAFE. CLEANING CREW ON THE WAY. WILL CONTINUE THE MISSION."

His cell phone silently vibrated. He removed it from his pocket and read the message, then responded. "SKOTOS"

He was summed to the office. He placed the cell phone back into his pocket and entered. "Yes, sir."

"Have you heard anything about DeLorean and his sister?"

He shook his head. "Nothing."

"Let me know when you do."
"I will."
"Thank you."

The conversation was abrupt, but before he left the office, he glanced at the man swivel his chair around and look out the window at the birds that flew gracefully above the cesspool of humanity.

Epilogue

The Aristocrat was not dead, and neither were his evil intentions. Albright had advanced to the next phase of his appointment that would thwart the sinister desires of the *Inner Sanctum* while preparing Bobby and Sergeant Martinez to enter a world of darkness never imagined. Marty would find meaning in the archives of Dr. Martinez's discovery.

Made in the USA
Columbia, SC
20 April 2023

2b87c594-a24e-4e53-b326-a8190698e776R01